Bowl of Night

Bowl of Night

A novel

Kathrin King Segal

Published by: Bucket List Books
First printing: September 2021
Cover Design by Robin Vuchnich
Interior Layout by Spiro Books
Author photo by Steve Kaplan

LIBRARY OF CONGRESS CATALOGUING-IN-PUBLICATION DATA:
Segal, Kathrin King

Bowl of Night/Kathrin King Segal—1st edition
ISBN: 978-0-9835181-3-6
Library of Congress Control Number: 2021936133

In memory of my friend,

Ina Rubinstein Sloan

AWAKE ! for Morning in the Bowl of Night
Has flung the Stone that puts the Stars to Flight:
And Lo ! the Hunter of the East has caught
The Sultan's Turret in a Noose of Light.

Rubáiyát of Omar Khayyám

Part I

1

*A*fter the long-running nudie musical closed, I found myself in need of funds, so I did some pick-up singing gigs around the city, which is how I met Harry Lamb. We spent much of the next eight months drinking and laughing and fucking our way through swank New York hotels, the ephemeral nights bleeding into anguished dawn partings when he dashed off to wherever his art dealing business took him.

And then he vanished.

I waited.

I am waiting.

His last note says, *"Will call tomorrow, already miss you."* It's been a week. Two weeks. A month. I'm not sure what to do.

He had mentioned the London auctions, the Paris galleries, but now his message service says that Mr. Lamb has "terminated." I only have the one number.

Forget about him, friends tell me: He must be married or maybe he's a polygamist or in witness protection. Or maybe dead.

Forget him? I am unmoored, a ghost drifting through the city, looking for him in all our old haunts. He's been ripped away like Velcro, leaving the ragged half exposed and raw.

I've never been out of the country, not even to Canada. But I could go to London. To Paris. I could just take off in search of Harry - and maybe a continental singing career. This seems like the sort of daring act that could, at the very least, make for good conversation later in life.

I want to get on a plane immediately but there's a lot to arrange. Illegally sublet my apartment or just move out? I get the name of a guy who'll sublet it on the down low. Every day that passes widens the gap of time and space between Harry and me.

So that's how I find myself, on the far end of 1972, on a half-empty, London-bound BOAC 707. The passengers are mostly Brits returning from a whiskey sales convention in New York. They pass bottles around, cheerfully, sloppily pouring single malt into the airline's plastic glasses. They're happy to share with me and I pretend to like it and play along with all the flirting. There's quite a bit of singing – "Scotland the Brave" and "England the Whatever" and multiple choruses of "God Save the Queen." A few hours into the flight, the salesmen begin to pass out like soldiers falling on a battlefield, leaving a sudden, jarring calm.

Outside the window, a trace of red sun – is it rising or setting? – lingers like a lipstick smudge on black velvet. I flip through the *International Herald Tribune*, landing on a story about the latest plane hijacking by the same loonies who shot up the Olympics a few months ago. I guess we all wonder, at one time or another, what we would do if faced with a choice of being heroes or just saving our own sorry asses. I'd like to think I would be the one who leaped in and took a risk, so I go with this fantasy; reasoning with the hijackers, convincing them that we are all caught up in the common human experience. There's a moment of calm in which I can already see the headlines: REBECCA BELL, 25-YEAR-OLD AMERICAN SINGER, FOILS IN-FLIGHT TERRORIST PLOT. Unfortunately, the movie-in-my-head takes a dark twist. The masked gunmen begin shooting us, one by one. The blood sprays into the air and slides red and thick down the windows. I want to go back to the happy ending but can't find my way.

This horribly skewed daydream makes my mouth go dry. I search in my purse for a stray mint and come across the absentee ballot I forgot to mail; my vote for George McGovern. Well, too late now.

The snoring Brits are somehow reassuring, at least until the plane begins to shiver and lurch and a guy across the aisle wakes up and heaves into his barf bag.

2

*L*ondon is in the grip of a dank early winter, the sun barely leaching through the morning gray. I'm too captivated by my new surroundings to even feel the cold. The fact that one can get into a flying thing and six hours later be in an entirely different country, seems miraculous to me, although this sense of wonder would wear off over the years. But that first time, as with most other first times, I am enthralled.

A musician I knew had scribbled down the name of the Queen Anne Guest House on Rose Street, near Regent's Park. It's a poky, narrow building with a faded sign: To let. In my jet-lagged, giddy mind, this looks like "toilet," so I'm laughing when I come face to face with the concierge. I calm down and ask about a room.

"Our last." She insinuates that getting a room here is akin to winning the lottery. "How long will you be staying?"

My turtleneck is tight and soiled from the long trip and I'm looking forward to a shower. "I'm not sure. A week or two?"

If I don't find him in London by then, well, I'll move on to Paris. Harry always said the French would like my songs. Yes, running off to be an expat artist is the worst kind of cliché but love will make you do dumb shit. And the idea of a country that speaks another language seems wildly adventuresome to me, a girl who grew up in the home-schooled hinterland of evangelical Christians.

The concierge pulls out a large key and leads the way. "You'll have to carry your own bags. I have a bad back."

She looks pretty fit to me. I follow her through a dark sitting room, up a narrow staircase to the attic. Shelves of dusty knickknacks, mostly ceramic turtles, line the landings. The stairs list slightly to the right. I sling the guitar over my shoulder. It's in a black vinyl case stuffed with clothes for extra cushioning.

"You're a musician?" she asks, breath puffing. "What sort of music?"

"Um… folk, mostly," I apologize. "Folksinger," which once projected an image of counter-cultural hipness now suggests warmed-over hippie. I've been told I have talent, but tend to snag myself on distractions like Harry, which is why, after some eight years in New York, I have little to show for it. I don't mention the nudie musical.

"Well, at least it's not that loud rubbish." She shows me the bathroom in the hall. There's a tub with quaint claw feet, and a sink. "Be sparing with the hot water and be sure to wash out the tub after you've used it. The loo is the next door down." More instructions about breakfast (between seven and eight-thirty, for an extra charge of half a crown, whatever that is), and coming in too late at night (don't). The chances are slim I will experience breakfast here.

After she leaves, I start to unpack. I found this suitcase in a thrift shop, and even though it's heavy and has cracks, I love the faded stickers from ancient destinations glued onto the beige herringbone surface. Whoever owned it sailed on the *Queen Mary* and the S.S. *Constitution*.

The room is tiny, and very quiet. An aged, dusty lamp on the night table puts out maybe twenty-five watts. I have a thousand watts of loneliness. It hits me like a rogue wave, and I know it well because I'm no stranger to strange rooms. My family was a transient horde of Good News bearers, led by my father, a preacher whose restlessness and passion for saving souls drove us ever onward. I believed all of it then;

the born again, sinful, god-fearing, speaking in tongues babble, and even though I came to reject it as a lot of fairy tales, it's still likely imprinted on my DNA.

I pull myself out of the downward spiral and head to the bathroom, which is large and freezing, with no source of heat save for a mysterious gas device that looks as if it might detonate. The tub seems clean, but I have to use a piece of toilet paper to pick out a wiry black hair. I fill it to the brim with steaming hot water. Amazing, a country that produced Shakespeare can't come up with a shower, but the bath is a blessing.

Sensual memories of Harry flow in. I know I'll find him wherever he is; London. Paris. The Himalayas. The anticipation mixed with uncertainty creates a pleasant hurt. As a child, I became obsessed with a packaged chocolate cupcake that had a cream center. It was the center I wanted most, but I always began the cupcake-eating ritual by licking around the edges, moving ever closer to the moment when I would plunge my tongue into the sugary cream, delaying the pleasure as long as possible.

How could I ever forget you? he once said. *I don't think that is actually possible.*

Apparently it was.

Hearing his voice in my head stirs a volatile mix of pain and rage. Oh, yes, I will find him. Even if it is just to send him to fiery hell.

Wilted from the bath, I collapse on the squishy bed, longing for sleep but too tormented by my decisions, if you can call them that; leaving the tenement walk-up in a tolerable Manhattan slum, and ditching my New York "career" – which, granted, consisted of singles bars and restaurant gigs and the occasional rich-people party – for the disorientation of foreign lands and the search for a man who may no longer want me.

Harry was at one of those posh parties; a New Year's Eve bash in an Upper East Side townhouse, at the very moment that 1971 turned into 1972 – ten nine eight seven six... I was at the microphone, willowy sexy in back-bearing black; long gold-red tresses. And there he is, Harrold

Doyle Lamb – could there be a more English name, with the two r's? – leaning against the bar, tall enough, muddy blondish hair and sleepy eyes, like he had just fallen out of bed, and a drink in hand, clearly not his first that night. Yet he was managing to carry off a bespoke tuxedo, collar loosened. After everyone finished the drunken mangling of "Auld Lang Syne," he asked me to sing "Fire and Rain."

We exchanged a few words. Up close, I could see he was on the near side of forty or maybe had lived hard enough to look older than his years. He liked my singing and he said he was an art dealer and had no real home base. I lived in the city but grew up all over. Our actual dialogue was spoken in pheromones. My body responded to Harry before the thought reached my conscious brain, turning me into malleable silk. He caressed my cheek, as if he were blind and learning me by touch. My eyes closed. The party roared around us but we were no longer there. He led me from the living room. The guests merely talking statues we passed by.

I had never fucked a man five minutes after I met him. Until then.

One of the guest bedrooms had a locking door. The bed, neatly made, covered by an embroidered quilt. I will always remember that quilt and its pockmarked submission beneath my skin. We kissed for the first time, a spinning sensation of a kiss and the taste of him was like an extension of myself, as if we had always been connected in some way and the coming together was just a formality. The sad truth was that until that night I had never come with a man. Or a woman. By myself, yes, a hundred times and more, so addicted to the sensation I discovered at a disconcertingly young age that I thought I was possessed by an evil spirit, and tried to quell it with prayer. *Oh Jesus, please deliver me,* but this only inflamed my clandestine domain, a place of dark dominance, in which I was both captive and master, mistress and slave. All of this smashed into that first time with Harry, because he was not to be deterred and my mind raced full force into that darkness, body following his direction, despite the slips and sorrys and do you prefers of any first time, and for once I was not watching myself from a distance or thinking but just feeling the hardness of him and the wet surrendering of myself under his hands and mouth. In this there is a sweet refrain of religious ecstasy, the kind I witnessed growing up.

You are baptized in Jesus, amen. The congregation on the riverbank echoes amen. Daddy holds the head of a disciple and bends him backward into the river, a split-second soul-cleansing. Mama, in her home-sewn, pale-blue shirtwaist, sings "Shall We Gather at the River," and the flock wades in, arms around one another. Down by the riverside, we sing. Wade in the water, children, God's gonna cover the water. The sun gleams down like a golden idol, somewhere in the heart of Missouri.

My father, Pastor Bell, preached with a fervor that teetered between brilliance and insanity. Mama played the rickety upright piano we dragged everywhere with us in a trailer behind the old Plymouth. The rest of the nomadic flock packed themselves into a blue Volkswagen van.

At fourteen, I had already begun to harbor doubts, knowing that I was supposed to feel awed by the power of God as He spoke through the mouths of mere mortals, but I was starting to think that they were all, well, kind of nuts. I held myself aloof as the worshipers reached that point of frenzy when they dropped to their knees, writhing on the ground and flopping like fish, mouths emitting rolling garbled sounds; the tongues of Babel straight from the Lord.

Didn't everybody's family worship this way, hollering and crying and falling about? Would God even listen if my father didn't entreat Him with all his passion and fury?

Adolescence hit me like Noah's flood. I loved Jesus. Jesus was my invisible friend, my childhood sweetheart, my confessor. He would always be there for me. Jesus loves me 'cause the Bible tells me so. But my new-found hormones yearned to cheat on Jesus. I sympathized with Mary – poor pregnant Mary! – a minor player with the evangelicals – who came up with what was *truly* the greatest story ever told and *got away with it.*

Unlike me, the little slut-in-waiting, my brother, Gideon, a year older, had the spirit in him and the voice of an angel. Life would deal him some bad cards, his sweetness souring until all that was left was righteous rage. He took off when he turned sixteen. Oh Gideon, Gideon. Maybe some people are born with the killing seed inside them. Maybe we both were.

All those years of morning prayer, evening prayer, Sunday meetings, songs, and celebration – it was, after all, a joyous, nomadic community of true believers – yet at seventeen, all I wanted was to slip away to meet the Brylcreemed teen cashier who winked at me in the Piggly Wiggly.

What do you think happened? Did those well-meaning people get the heavenly rewards they deserved? Or did my parents' rusty Plymouth slip into a ravine one icy Arkansas night when they were on their way back to camp from a pray-in, tired and gratified from bringing the Lord to the lost? Does God have a sense of humor or what? Where the hell was He?

At the moment the Plymouth flew into the air, I was donating my virginity to the cashier, in the ripped back seat of his Studebaker. And Gideon was long gone. How odd that we both were chosen to live, along with the rest of the flock who were crammed into a VW van some two hundred yards behind the flying Plymouth.

That was the moment I began to turn away from god – lowercase – for good, when everyone said how it was "god's will" and they were "in a better place" and "god loved them so much he called them early" and all I could think was, *Fuck god.*

A few days later, after the burials and tears, numb with grief and weighted down with a rock of survivor guilt I tried to kick into the smallest corner of my mind, I hitched to New York. It was nineteen sixty-five! I knew absolutely nothing about life in the big city. Or much of anything else. My "education" consisted of Bible studies, the occasional foray into a new school when the truant officers came around, or sneaking into some local library. I was a blank slate with a hunger to learn about... everything. I had to drown out the Bible quotes, the

Psalms, Matthew and John and Paul and all the rest of them. I replaced them with John and Paul and George and Ringo.

I had to break up with Jesus, although we would remain friends.

After kicking around New York for a few years, catching the tail end of the folk craze in Greenwich Village, and joining and quitting a few bands that aspired to mediocrity, I heard about an audition for *Au Naturel!* a new theater musical seeking actors willing to perform in the buff. If there is anything that prepares you for shedding your clothes on stage, it is a renounced religious background.

By some quirk of fate, all this led me to Harry Lamb.

3

The next afternoon, I set out to explore London. And, of course, find Harry. In my naiveté, I expect this will be as simple as making a few phone calls or just summoning him up by virtue of desire. Harry had promised to take me here for the auctions. We'd stay at the Connaught, the classiest hotel. We'd touch each other under the crisp white tablecloths in the tearoom.

The Connaught seems like a good place to start.

With an Underground map in hand, bestowed by the landlady, I make my way from the St. Johns Wood station to Bond Street. London is not quite as I imagined, my preconceptions forged by too much Sherlock Holmes and Charles Dickens and Jack the Ripper. No fog. No begging urchins. A glint of sun sneaks like a knife between the trees of Grosvenor Square and vanishes into an early night as I approach the stately hotel. I try to look as if I belong, reminding myself that some ancestor on my mother's side was supposedly an illegitimate English aristocrat. The tearoom is decorated with gleaming sterling and flowers and the finest linens. The fragrance of brewed tea and fresh-baked scones reminds me how terribly hungry I am.

My body freezes in place when I see him. He has his back to me and is getting up from a table on the far side of the room. I know that unruly hair, and the gray, belted raincoat. Is it possible? I take a step toward him, and in that encapsulated instant, every detail of the affair, foolish start to mysterious finish, every sexual high and emotional low, flashes like a kaleidoscope in my brain...

He exits through the hotel lobby. I run after him.

Stately black taxis line the street in front of the hotel. One is just pulling away. I see the man's profile.

Of course it isn't Harry, you idiot. There must be dozens of men on this block alone with the identical raincoat.

On the barest hope, I ask the desk clerk. "Do you have a Harrold Lamb staying here?"

He checks, shakes his head. "Sorry, Miss." His eyes linger on me. I'm so out of place in this high-class hotel, with the impeccably dressed clientele. I slip out the door, still the girl who never quite fit in. Who was perpetually saying goodbye.

I know how to lose people; in fact, I excel at it. Moving from place to place, we always left stuff behind. The cat I loved when I was six. Our van pulled away from the house where we'd packed up so quickly because we were heading....someplace else. Someplace better, my father said, where there were more people that needed him. The Lost. The Unsaved. Sinners. Jews. I screamed that we had forgotten Daisy. Papa pressed the accelerator, lurching us forward onto the road. Mom assured me that the next tenants would feed Daisy and, besides, cats don't like to travel. I pictured Daisy waiting for me to come home, wondering why I had left her, and I began to cry, feeling as if I were Daisy, abandoned in the endless silence of an empty house.

Despite all the cats and clothes and dolls and houses and humans left behind in a trail of memory rubble, nothing has prepared me for losing Harry, for the visceral blow to my sense of balance and order in the universe. Is it because I never grieved properly for my family, and Harry is merely the sum of collective mourning? I don't know, but there is a hole in time and space that I am floating through. Perhaps this is why I refuse to let it go. I'm no longer a small, helpless child in a rattling van, driven by a fanatical father. This time I will not let my treasure go, even if it is a futile quest.

After a few blocks of aimless walking, I come to a pub, softly lit with old-fashioned gaslight-style lamps, and crowded with men sipping amber beer from tall, thick mugs. I order scotch, and then remember they call it whiskey and that I don't like it, and carry it to a small corner table. The whiskey quickly does its job, tinting the room in softer hues. "Is there a telephone?" I ask the bartender.

He calls me "Luv" and points to an ancient booth in the back.

In the rubble at the bottom of my purse, there's a smudged business card: Alistair Nelson. The Nelson Gallery. Old Bond Street. W1S.

I remember the first time I heard Alistair Nelson's name. Harry had taken me to a New York Sotheby's auction and led me through the exhibition rooms; a quickie course in art history. He pointed out details in the paintings I never would have noticed – the arrangement of cherubs, the tilt of an arm, the artist's sly ridicule of a pompous toff. He pointed out a Dante Rossetti portrait of a woman with hair like mine; long, tangled, reddish curls. "Pre-Raphaelite," he said. "You are the reincarnation. I think that's why I fell in love with you."

"You mean it wasn't my brilliant singing?"

"That was nice but it was your naked back and the way the light fell on your hair."

"Too bad we met after *Au Naturel!* You would have fallen for more than my naked back."

"Ah, but I did see you in *Au Naturel!*"

My breath caught at the thought of him being in the audience, a stranger to me then. Me on stage with the rest of the cast, all naked for the world to see.

"So you were the guy in the front row with the binoculars." There really were many of these.

"Now why didn't I think of that?"

We kissed, the Rossetti model watching us.

In front of a small picture signed by one of Rembrandt's contemporaries, Harry leaned in close and whispered, "From the school of Alistair Nelson."

"What do you mean? Who is Alistair Nelson?"

"I mean," Harry explained with a sly grin, "that the signature or the provenance was in some doubt, until my pal Alistair provided it. Buyers like a signature, so believe me, there are quite a number of 'Lambs' around."

"He forged it? You've done it, too?"

He put his finger to my lips. "'Forged' is such a harsh word."

I confess I felt a *frisson* of exhilaration that he might be involved in something illicit, even dangerous.

Provenance (I looked it up later): from the French, provenir: to come forth; originate. The history of ownership of a valued object or work of art. I also looked up pre-Raphaelite.

That night we enjoyed a late dinner with Alistair Nelson, a London gallery-owner in his fifties, tall and slim, with a wave of silver hair. Alistair laughed and drank and talked in equal measure. We were at a crazy Greek restaurant in Greenwich Village that had a band and indulged the Greek tradition of smashing plates. All three of us, rather drunk, got into the spirit, hurling glassware to the floor in time to the music. After the long dinner, Harry was hailing a cab when Alistair pressed his business card into my hand. "Next time you're in London, my dear." I didn't let on that I had never really been anywhere.

Now, I dial the number on Alistair's card. The rings are harsh double bursts.

"Nelson Gallery."

I ask for Alistair, and give my name. He probably doesn't even remember me. I'm about to hang up when Alistair's crisp voice comes on the line.

"Rebecca? How nice to hear from you." He has the generic tone of someone who has no idea how he knows me.

"I'm Harry Lamb's...friend. We met in New York last winter."

"Of course! Rebecca. That Greek restaurant with you and Harry. My, what a madhouse, all those broken plates! I guess you could say it was a smashing time."

His good cheer is infectious and encouraging. "I'm here in London now. Just for a few days. I'm looking for – I'm just looking around."

"Lovely!" he says. "It would be a delight to see you. And excellent timing! We're preparing an opening for tomorrow night. A little cocktail thingie here at the gallery. Please come by if you're free and you don't mind being bored by a bunch of stuffy old art hounds."

"Hmm, you make it sound so appealing."

"No broken plates, I promise!"

I want to ask him about Harry but it seems so desperate, and Alistair is still talking.

"You sing, as I recall. The expat artist! I suppose Americans will be fleeing like fleas after all that election business. Getting that Nixon person again. Your country is a constant source of surprise and amusement to us over here. I hope I'm not being too presumptuous."

"No, no." But I feel a stir of patriotic resentment. You can say bad things about your own country – or family – but you don't want to hear an outsider say those same things, no matter how true.

"One moment," Alistair says. I hear muffled voices, then he's back. "Between five and seven."

"Excuse me?"

"The opening."

"Yes, of course. I'll be there."

4

*A*listair's party is in full swing, clearly visible through the high, wide windows of the gallery; a crush of bodies, laughing, chatting, drinking the free Glenfiddich and scarfing down the buffet. In a corner by the door, a large copper stand overflows with black umbrellas, like a brace of fallen crows dripping onto a sheaf of soggy *London Times.*

I remove my coat, the chic Betsey Johnson that Harry bought me, a body-hugging, ankle-length chocolate brown, of fine, soft wool. My dress is a long, bias-cut, pale-blue jersey that features a high Victorian collar. Brown-suede lace-up boots with impractical platform heels make me taller than my five foot seven. I'm also wearing heavy silver snake rings on each hand. Yes, I like to blend in.

Alistair deals in Renaissance Old Masters but this evening he's showcasing a rising contemporary artist, a sculptor with a peculiar collection of bronze nudes and mythological creations with an erotic bent. I wander through the crowd to the open bar, grab a gin and tonic and some fishy hors d'oeuvres and try to look at ease.

Silver-fox Alistair is in conversation with a small group. Around the collar of a crisp, white Oxford shirt, he sports a wool tartan tie of muted reds and blues.

"Rebecca, my dear, lovely to see you." The other women mostly wear stodgy wool suits and sweaters. There is a distinct aroma of damp sheep about the room. To his other guests, Alistair announces, "Rebecca was in *Au Naturel!* on Broadway."

This elicits a predictable ripple of interest. One woman says, "Oh yes, that played in London. I didn't see it."

A ruddy-nosed man adds, with a leer, "I did! Wasn't it chilly in those drafty old theaters?" He laughs, as if he is the first person to have ever come up with this.

"One of the great regrets of my life," Alistair states, "was not getting to see la belle Rebecca in *Au Naturel!*"

Another woman joins the group. She is short, with a doughy, inquisitive face, dark hair pulled back in a bun, and wearing a burgundy, knee-length wool dress. Her necklace is a delicate spray of diamonds and rubies.

"My wife, Agnes. Dear, this is Rebecca, Harry Lamb's… friend from the States."

"How do you do?" She extends a hand. I notice the trace of another accent behind the clipped English words. Agnes draws her husband aside and whispers in his ear. She stares at me, and leaves the room.

Unsettled, I drift off to study the bronzes. The sculptor, a thin man with a bony face and long, greasy, black hair, holds court a few feet away. His work tends toward the grotesque. The female nudes have limp breasts that look as if they've been sucked dry; the male figures' penises are long and deformed, sometimes coiling into snakeheads or disappearing up their own anuses. Why would anyone want to buy this crap? After a while, the barrage of teeth, fangs, contorted genitals, and multifold sexuality drives me out of the room.

After freshening up in the bathroom I really don't want to return to the party, but the thought of the sad little hotel fills me with dread.

There are several closed doors in the corridor. I try one, but it's locked. The next is a broom closet. The third door opens into a tasteful sitting room, unsurprisingly filled with works of art. Large paintings, in ornate gilt frames, are stacked against the walls. In one, angels dance attendance on a fleshy naked Venus. Across the room, a martyred Jesus bleeds from thorns and a gaping hole in his side. My childhood Jesus wasn't all torn up and bloody. We preferred him healthy and attractive. We didn't care much about Mary, preferring to avoid the whole "virgin" discussion.

I sink down onto a sofa, fingering one of the silk-damask throw pillows. A radio plays the faint strains of Satie's *Gymnopaedie #1*. The paintings' towering images press closer, their pain and pleasure sinking into my skin. There's a faint, familiar cologne. It's almost as if Harry has just been in this very room. I usually don't like men's cologne, but Harry's had a tangy, subtle aroma that became erotically entangled in my brain. Some kind of custom blend. Not likely Alistair would wear it. I pick up one of the throw pillows and take a whiff. No, must be my imagination. I rise and cross the room to study one of the paintings. It is old, with a webby cracked surface, faded in places, showing an unselfconscious, quite naked, and plump young woman holding a bunch of green grapes. She has long reddish hair like mine. I kneel down to study the signature. From the school of Alistair Nelson? The school of Harry Lamb? Harry would know all about the provenance…

"Rebecca." Alistair is standing in the doorway.

I jump up. "Sorry, I didn't mean to invade your privacy. It just got a little warm in there."

"No harm done. I see you were admiring my Titian."

I remember, with a blush, when I'd first viewed one of the artist's paintings and Harry had to correct my pronunciation, with a delighted laugh: "*Tee*-shin, not TIT-ee-an."

That's what comes of getting your education in an evangelical school of art-is-the-devil's-work.

"Not mine, of course," Alistair says, bringing me back to the present.

19

"Goes on the block at Sotheby next month." He straightens one of the paintings on the wall, then two more.

"I can't imagine having these lying around the house. 'Should I sell the Van Gogh this week or keep it?'"

He chuckles. "Yes, there are worse problems."

The music ends. A crisp BBC announcer reports that the mastermind behind the terrorist attacks at the Munich Olympics has been identified—

Alistair switches off the radio.

"I'm wondering," I begin, "if you've, well, if you've seen Harry." My face flushes and I wish I could take the words back.

"Harry? Hmm, it's been a while…let me think." He adjusts a few more wall paintings. "Went to Paris last I heard."

Paris.

"Oh that's interesting. I was thinking of going to Paris." Well, now I am. "Singing, you know."

"Wonderful idea! I hope you find our Harry."

"If I only knew where to start."

He shows his crooked teeth in a smile. "Chris Fargate! You must look him up! He has a gallery, used to be married to a French girl. Knows absolutely everyone, people in the music business, too. He and Harry were drinking buddies as I recall." He opens a drawer and rummages around. "I've his number somewhere. Be right back."

When he fails to return right away, I wonder if I misunderstood. Was I supposed to follow? The hall is empty. I can hear low voices behind a closed door.

A door snaps open, like a gunshot.

"Here we are!" Alistair hands me a folded piece of paper. "Chris Fargate Gallery. But be warned, Fargate is quite the skirt-chaser."

"I think I can take care of myself."

"I'm sure you can." He regards me, as if he's trying to make a decision. Then: "Oh, and I had the most wonderful idea! Well, it was actually my wife's idea. There's this little gift we've been meaning to ship off to Fargate but keep forgetting. Perhaps you could do me the very great favor of bringing it to him? It would give you a good excuse to get together. And then perhaps my dear Agnes will stop nagging me about it."

"Well…okay. What is it?"

Alistair gives a short laugh, "I forgot how blunt you Americans are."

"I didn't mean to be nosy."

"No, no, no, not at all. It's just a little, what do the Jews say? 'Tchotchke.'"

The way he says "Jews" makes me think of picking up a dead bug with a wad of paper. Perhaps he doesn't like Jews. I have to confess I never met one until I moved to New York, where I discovered they are much the same as everyone else, if perhaps a bit more talkative.

"Of course," Alistair adds, "we'll pay you for your trouble." He exits again, a moment later reappearing with a narrow box, just under a foot long, tightly wrapped in brown paper and tied with white string. "See? It won't take up much space in your suitcase." The box is heavier than it appears. "And here, my dear." He reaches into his jacket, removes his wallet, and presses some bills into my hand.

"No, that's not really…" I take it anyway. My savings are already running low, and the truth is that I'm used to men handing me money; tips for singing, cab fare, powder room cash, "get yourself something" money. Yet this seems to burn my hand. I'm about to hand it back, along with the box, but Alistair gives my shoulder an avuncular squeeze.

"I'd love to chat with you longer but I have a gallery full of colleagues." He adds in a stage whisper, "Most of whom I can't stand." He looks me in the eyes. "Good luck to you, Rebecca. My regards to Harry if you catch up with him."

5

This is the cheapest way to get from London to Paris; train to Dover, ferry to Calais, bus to Paris. Cheaper than flying. Cheaper than the Hovercraft. Easier than swimming.

The English Channel is a roller coaster of choppy gray waves. At French Customs, multiple inspectors rummage through the baggage. There's been some new threat from Black September. A young Swiss couple, their long, downy legs unseasonably bare beneath hiking shorts, unstrap their backpacks and thunk them onto the metal table.

I place my guitar and suitcase on the counter. Alistair's package is buried deep inside.

The customs inspector asks me something in French. I shake my head. He gives an impatient shrug. "Food? Plants?"

"What? Oh, no, no." I really don't know what's in the box. I barely know Alistair. I do my best to smile and act the American bimbo. Certainly, the thing isn't alive or edible – is it? – or valuable, or why else would Alistair have entrusted it to me? But could it contain… drugs? Jewels? Holy shit, what have I gotten myself into? I can see the gendarmes carting me off to jail, and my not speaking the language and being sentenced to Devil's Island.

The inspector calls over a man in a uniform. I oh-so-casually take out a lipstick and apply it in a small mirror, but have to stop because my hand is shaking. They speak rapidly, looking at me. The first man unzips the guitar case, revealing the clothes stuffed inside around the guitar. He feels around and zips it shut. The other man shrugs and walks back to his post. The inspector stamps my passport. "Bienvenue à France, mademoiselle."

I go to the rest room and splash cold water on my face.

A short time later the bus is jouncing along the dark roads of Normandy in moonlight, a highway bordered by miles of small white crosses, thousands of identical grave markers that seem to glow in the dark, stretching back over the low hills and vanishing into the night. For a while, I study *Teach Yourself French* in the bus's dim light. At least I know some pronunciation from listening to Jacques Brel and Edith Piaf records over and over, although that probably gives me an accent that is a mix of Belgian and Parisian brothel. The bus driver turns off the interior lights and we are all in the dark.

I doze off into a dream that I'm in Daddy's old Plymouth, squashed between my mom and my brother Gideon. We're singing "You Are My Sunshine" when there is a squeal of brakes, the car swerves, and we are falling into space –

My head bumps against the window. I'm surprised to find that I'm on a bus in the French countryside. At a rest stop, I groggily follow the other passengers into a café. I ask for *cafe au lait* and *pain au chocolat*. They are so delicious I want to cry, to share this delight with someone. But the French words won't come; all I have is a muddle of trite tourist phrases and song lyrics. I have been struck deaf and mute.

The proprietors of the inn are a squat, rosy couple, like an illustration out of some fairy tale or an old Flemish painting. An emaciated man in the corner plays the concertina while the bus driver, the proprietors, and several of the passengers dance around, hands on each other's waists. I can scarcely keep from laughing aloud. Harry would so enjoy this bizarre little moment! An old man hands me a glass of red wine. I must be very tired because it hits me like a heavy drug. The music swirls around me and all at once I am dancing, too. The old man grips my waist and laughs, his mouth a dark lake of missing teeth.

The bus pulls up at the Gare du Nord at three-thirty on Sunday morning. I'm not sure how I even got back on the bus, and I quickly check to see that all my possessions are with me and intact. They are. The tourist assistance booth and the currency exchange are closed and I have no way of turning my American dollars and British pounds into francs or cashing a traveler's check. The Metro stopped running at midnight. The cavernous terminal is chilled and drafty. I drag the suitcase and guitar to the taxi stand.

"Je voudrais aller a l'Hotel Paradis, uh, quatre rue Griseille, s'il vous plait," I tell one of the drivers, quite proud of having assembled this sentence, and add, "Quinzième Arrondissement."

The London concierge turned out to be a wealth of information. She'd lived in Paris for several years and gave me the name of a small hotel. She went into some detail explaining the "arrondissement" arrangement of Paris districts, with the little hotel located in the fifteenth, and she helped me put a call through to reserve a room. As I was checking out, she handed me a much-traveled *Plan de Paris* guide, each page of the little red book detailing an arrondissement, with an attached map of the Metro. She also wrote down the address of the "Alliance Française," a non-matriculated French-language school "right in the middle of the artsy part of the city." She sighed, "I envy you. There's nothing more wonderful than to be young and in Paris."

The taxi driver snaps, "Comment?"

It sounds like "common" and I wonder if it's an insult. I repeat the address, slowly. "J'ai, um... American dollars et Anglaise. Quel est le prix du taxi?"

"Quatre cents francs."

Four cents? That can't be right. Forty? No, that is "quarante." Four *hundred?* At five francs to the dollar, a franc is twenty cents…math was never my best subject. "Quatre cents francs?"

He yawns.

I drag my stuff back into the terminal. The huge clock on the wall measures the passing of five slow minutes.

"Bonsoir, mademoiselle. Comment ça va?" The man is wiry, with dark, long-lashed eyes. His tight jeans are topped by a faded leather jacket. "Vous-êtes Américaine?"

"Oui. Parles anglais?"

He grins. I have no idea if that means yes or no, but I explain, in English, the encounter with the cab driver.

"Comment?"

I realize that this is the French equivalent of "huh?" "Hotel. Pour moi. Taxi. Expensive. Très, uh, cher. Très cher." I rub my thumb and first two fingers together as illustration.

"Ah! Je comprend. Mais non, non, non! Pas l'hôtel çe soir!" He purses his lips. "Eet ees late, comprend? You come my flat. Tonight. Okay?"

There is darkness in his eyes. His hands restlessly twirl an unfiltered cigarette. A musty odor of stale tobacco and sweat wafts from his body.

"Uh, no, merci. I. Will. Stay. Here."

"Ici?" He gives a disdainful sniff. "Le Gard du Nord? Ç'est dangere-use." As he walks away, he calls back over his shoulder. "Folle Américaine!"

"Fuck you, too," I mutter.

(When I look it up later, I discover that he'd only called me crazy.)

"Taxi?" A chubby, mustached man with a driver's cap points to the doorway, where a cab stands empty. "Hotel Paradis. Allez!" He picks up my bag and guitar. I start to grab them back but he dashes off and stuffs them into a small, low-slung cab. After I climb in, four men squeeze in next to me. I'm pressed in on both sides, unable to escape. The car lurches forward, throwing me back against the seat as we tear out of the parking area. The men talk fast and loudly amongst themselves. As the cab careens around a corner, I'm squashed against the body of the man on my left. They are probably going to take me to a strange place and rape and kill me, but I'm too exhausted to process this or fight my way out of the car. How foolish this is. I would never do anything this stupid in America, but travel seems to bring out different rules, as if I have some kind of foreigner's protective shield, ridiculous as this sounds.

We rattle over a bridge. The Eiffel Tower looms in the distance. All this would be beautiful if I weren't terrified. They hand around a paper bag of pastries. Are they going to drug me? But they seem cheerful and chatty. I catch the words "steak" and "football" as the bumpy little car speeds through a residential area, down small streets. The car pulls to a halt, jolting us all forward. The driver and his friends clamber out and hand over my suitcase and guitar. One of the men rings the doorbell of a small, attached house with a sign on the front:

Hotel Paradis.

A woman in curlers and a bathrobe opens the door. She scolds the driver, squinting at me over his shoulder.

"Ma soeur," the driver explains. His sister. The woman pinches his cheek and says something teasing. I fumble in my bag for money.

"Non, non, pas d'argent!" the driver insists. He and his friends are already back inside the cab. "Bienvenue à Paris!" he calls out as they rattle off down the empty street.

6

The room at the Hotel Paradis is even smaller than the one in London, if that is possible, with a narrow bed and a sink with a rusty mirror over it. There are very likely prison cells with more space. A wooden wardrobe stands against the wall opposite the bed. The window is covered by a threadbare pull-shade that tap-tap-taps as puffs of cold air push it forward and back. Four flights below, a cobblestone courtyard leads to a street lined with attached row houses. If I lean out dangerously far and look to the left, I can see the glowing erector-set tip of the Eiffel Tower. I am instantly in love with Paris.

I unpack, and there is Alistair's box. After about a second of thinking it over, I unknot the string and carefully unfold the brown paper. Inside, wrapped in thick cotton, is a figurine, a reptile-like creature about eight inches high and made of smooth-polished black stone; marble or onyx. Not quite a lizard, nor a snake, but something in between. It stands upright on a wide, scaled tail, its body spiraling to a small, intelligent, cat-like face, the eyes a glittering blue glass. The stone feels warm to the touch, as if it's absorbed the heat from decades of human hands. The letters Z A N D are etched into the base and under that the numbers: 25-3. March 1925? That would be about right for its hint of Art Nouveau design.

I stroke the stone body and look at its little face. The blue eyes glow and flicker, as though reflecting a shifting of light in the room. The stone heats up, to the point that I drop the figurine onto the bed, lest it burn my hand. It stares at me.

Unnerved, I touch it with a fingertip to test its temperature. When it is cool enough to handle, I replace the figurine in the box, carefully rewrap it, and bury it under clothes in the open suitcase.

Life looks a little clearer in the morning. The concierge lets me use the phone in the lobby to call Chris Fargate. At the mention of Alistair Nelson and a package, he suggests I stop by in the afternoon.

If I'm going to get any gigs, I need an agent. I used to know a guy who transferred from the New York office of the Solomon Morgan Talent Agency to the Paris branch. With the help of the *Plan de Paris*, I figure out how to get to the Right Bank.

Unlike the more democratic New York subways, the Paris Metro has a caste system. I buy a second-class ticket but there's no one in the first-class car, which has nice upholstered red seats, so at the next stop I change cars. A conductor passes through and stares as I silently practice my defense: *Oh really? I didn't know. I'm just an American.*

I exit the Metro at Étoile. The Solomon Morgan Agency is in an elegant nineteenth-century townhouse, the reception area hushed by thick carpets. The receptionist, who seems insulted by my very existence, informs me that the New York agent left the company with no forwarding information. Besides, they don't take on new talent and only handle the European business of signed clients.

Well, thank you and fuck you.

In a tiny cafe, I order an omelet and a crusty baguette and a hot chocolate with whipped cream. I look at my list:

1. Chris Fargate
2. agent
3. French school
4. Harry

Finding a missing man should be a snap compared to trying to get a talent agent.

The Alliance Française is on Boulevard Raspail in the 7th Arrondissement. A familiar school aroma flashes me back to all the nervous first days and the crisp, unsullied notebooks and not-yet-chewed pencils, sharpened and ready. I knew my days at each school were numbered because we'd just move on to the next town or state, and the authorities would come around again and force my parents to enroll me into yet another school.

The murmurs from the classrooms mingle in a pleasant din. I hear a guitar coming from a small room. The musician finishes his piece, looks up, and sees me in the doorway. There are two people with him – a plump, dark-haired woman in her late twenties and a younger Asian man.

"I heard the music. I mean, j'attend la guitare—"

"That's okay, we speak English." He has the kind of face that is almost handsome but misses in some indefinable way. His features are even, his eyes a light brown and just a bit close together. Long sideburns blend up into a sandy Jew-fro.

"You're American?"

"I guess *you* are," the woman says. She wears round granny glasses and a smock-style long dress.

"She could be Canadian." The guitar player looks me over.

"Uh-uh. If she were Canadian, she'd have a great big *maple leaf* somewhere on her clothing so that everyone would know she *isn't* American."

"Hello, I'm in the room."

"Sorry." The musician laughs. It turns out he's from New York. Well, Queens. He puts out his hand. "Max Hurwitz."

The woman, Ellen, is from Brooklyn Heights, an expensive part of the borough. Jimmy hails from Hong Kong and is in Paris on a student-exchange program.

Max strums the opening chords of "Malagueña." I hum along, and then sing in full voice. When the song ends, Ellen asks, "So, what are you doing in *Paris*?" She has a way of emphasizing words as if she's trying to get a slightly sarcastic point across.

"I came here to meet New Yorkers. I wondered where they all went." I tell them about the strange taxi drivers. No one is familiar with the Hotel Paradis.

"Maybe it's not really *there*," Ellen says. "Whoever heard of the *French* being so *help*ful?"

Max plunks out the *Twilight Zone* theme on the guitar and they laugh, except for Jimmy. Ellen explains the joke.

Max says, "So I guess you'll be taking classes?"

"Are you studying here?"

"Just your basic French for foreigners." He explains that he was a lawyer at a big corporate firm and had an epiphany that if he didn't get away now he never would, so he "went expat." I guess that he's in his early thirties, although he has a boyish look that makes him seem younger. "At least I can always tell my grandchildren that I lived in Paris," he finishes.

"So why are *you* in Paris?" Ellen repeats.

I'm running after a man. "I want to try to sing here, and around Europe."

"Watch *out* for the Algerian men," Ellen says.

"Oh, come on," Max scoffs, "that's just a myth."

"Uh-*uh*. There's a *white slave trade* out of Paris to the Middle East."

I look from one to the other. "This is a joke, right?"

Max rolls his eyes. "*Yes*. This is the equivalent of the snipe hunt back home."

Then Jimmy wants to know what a snipe hunt is, and they talk amongst themselves.

I head out. Max catches up with me in the hall. "I've got a class but I was going to eat in the cafeteria after. It's really cheap, the best buy in town."

"I can't tonight. But maybe tomorrow."

"Oh. Okay. Maybe I'll see you around." He touches my arm lightly, the first physical contact I've had in a long time. It almost hurts.

7

The Christopher Fargate Gallery is on a small street tucked away in the mainly residential, comfortably bourgeois 16th near the Bois de Boulogne. The reception desk is deserted, so I venture into the main room, and browse through an exhibit of Middle Eastern artifacts. A catalogue explains that the works of art include miniature paintings by several late nineteenth-century Persian artists. The exhibit also features a wall of photographs, collected by Mr. Fargate during his travels through Turkey, Iran, and Iraq over a period of some twenty years.

"Très charmant, n'est-ce pas?" He's in his early forties, paunchy, thinning brown hair streaked with gray and in need of a trim. He has the look of someone who dresses hurriedly, in expensive clothes he takes for granted.

"Mr. Fargate?" His smile reveals typically askew English teeth. Alistair called him a womanizer but this man looks like a harmless academic.

"I'm Rebecca Bell. I called earlier. Alistair Nelson gave me your name when I was in London. I'm in Paris now."

"I can see that." He lights a cigarette, one of the short, brown French brands, and offers me one.

"No thanks."

The bell over the door gives a soft clunk as someone enters. Fargate watches the woman browse through his exhibit. Her dark hair is partly covered by a beige silk headscarf.

"Excuse me, Miss Bell." He approaches the woman with a few words in French. They cross the carpeted room and disappear into a private office. A few moments later, they emerge, the woman carrying a shopping bag from the department store Bon Marché. From the way she holds it, the bag seems to contain a heavy object. Chris Fargate opens the door and watches her walk down the street.

"Business," he says with a rueful smile. "But I can't complain. So you're a friend of Alistair's."

"Well, we just met a few times. Through Harry Lamb."

A pause. "Harry Lamb." There's a note of disdain.
"I heard he was in Paris."

Fargate shrugs. "I've seen him around. He likes Harry's Bar. Probably thinks it was named after him."

"Recently?"

"No, I don't think it was recent. I really couldn't say."

Harry's New York Bar is legendary. George Gershwin composed *An American in Paris* at the piano, or at least that's the story. It was the center of artsy 1920s and 1930s Paris.

Another customer enters. Chris Fargate says, "Sorry, Miss Bell…"

"Rebecca."

"Do people call you Becky?"

"No." I take the package out of my bag. "This is the… thing from Alistair."

He is expressionless as he puts it in a drawer and locks it. "Tell you what, let's meet for drinks later. Six? At Harry's Bar? Maybe you'll find your friend. Although I rather hope you don't. I'd prefer to have you all to myself."

8

Entering Harry's New York Bar, you pass a long, polished mahogany bar and matching walls, decorated with old photos, plaques, and other memorabilia. The mood is loud, animated, but there's an effortless chic about the French patrons, a contrast to the fat, louder tourists, Eurotrash, and businessmen in suits and ties. I can't help but envy the effortless style of the French. One woman, chic as a mannequin framed in a cigarette haze, wears drop-waisted gray satin slacks and an off-shoulder peasant blouse. She's smoking and leaning in close to a ruggedly handsome man in a black leather bomber jacket, who looks very much like the French film star Jean-Paul Belmondo.

I scan every face for my Harry.

Chris waves from a booth in the back. I make my way to his table. He stands, offering his face for the double air kiss.

"What would you like to drink?"

I'm trying to think of what a sophisticated Frenchwoman would order.

"Kir?" he suggests.

"Yes, that's fine."

"Did you notice the celebrity in our midst?" He nods toward the man in the leather bomber jacket. It really *is* Jean Paul Belmondo.

The waiter brings the drinks. Kir turns out to be white wine tinted with crème de cassis, giving it a crimson blush and a sweet tang. Chris is working on his second or third whiskey, nattering on about the art world and his Persian collection. I periodically get a whiff of his Scotch-tinged breath. Only twenty minutes have passed. A song floats in the background of the bar chatter, emerging in fragments:

"*La neige tombe sur la mer... C'est la fin de l'affaire*", a male singer laments, against a sweeping, romantic orchestral arrangement. I don't understand the words but the mood is exactly how I'm feeling.

"*... les oiseaux-lyres ont oublié comment chanter...*"

"What a strange and beautiful song."

Chris leans in, his lips grazing my hair, translating. "'Snow falls on the sea. It's the end of the affair. Lyrebirds have forgotten how to sing.'"

"What are leer birds?"

"I haven't the slightest."

"Some things sound better in French."

"*Most* things sound better in French."

"*....la neige tombe sur la mer...*"

"Do you want to go to bed with me?" he asks, with no more expression than if he were asking me to pass the salt.

"If I say no, do I have to pay for the drinks?"

He laughs. "I like you, Rebecca. Let me know if there's anything you need."

The list is too long. "You don't happen to know any agents, do you? I thought I had someone but apparently he heard I was coming and fled the country. Alistair mentioned you know people in the music business."

"You mean a talent agent? As a matter of fact, I do. Not that he's any kind of a big deal. I know he books dancers into the Pigalle. Alistair mentioned that you were in that 'scandalous' show." He winks.

"I was. In New York."

"Sorry I missed it. It played here but didn't last long. The Parisians are too jaded. I've always wondered, if you don't mind me asking. Did the actors ever get, uh, aroused?"

"What do you think?"

He signals for another drink. "If you change your mind about sleeping with me, the offer's still good."

"You were saying about the agent?"

"He comes in from time to time, likes Art Deco: Erte, Icart. I probably have his number back at the gallery. Armand Frochot. A peculiar fellow but he can probably help you. He books all over the world."

"I appreciate it. And Harry Lamb? Have you seen him?"

"Lover?"

"Well…"

"Haven't seen him. Sorry." He drains his whiskey and drapes one arm over my shoulder, the kind of move a teenager uses on a first date. The room is more crowded than when I arrived, but Jean Paul Belmondo is gone. People stand three deep at the bar. Everyone seems to be in high spirits, laughing and talking with friends.

I am with them, but not of them. The French chatter brings back my deaf-mute feeling. Every time I try to speak French, someone says, no no no I speak English, and their English is better than my bad French.

I slip out from under his arm.

"When will I see you again, Becky?"

I want to say "never," but I know so few people here. One day, maybe I won't have to trade off pieces of myself – or it will be too late, and I'll have chipped and sliced myself into nonexistence. I write the number of the Hotel Paradis on a cocktail napkin and give it to Chris.

He kisses me on both cheeks. "We'll get you an agent and a singing job, and then you'll be all set."

"I do have to go. And if you hear anything about Harry Lamb…"

He looks older; a disappointed man in a bar. "You're a lovely girl, Becky. I'll ask around about Harry. Could be anywhere, right? Here.

London. He had some dealings in Iran, I think. Or was it Iraq? No, Iran, I'm sure. It's a big world."

9

The following morning, a rude gust of wind shoves me through the door of a large, bland office building off the Champs Élysée. I take the elevator to the ninth floor and walk a long, echoing corridor to number 1106: "Agence Thèâtre et Spectacle. Armand Frochot." No one answers my knock but there is light behind the opaque glass, so I enter into a small waiting area. Posters of old-fashioned nightclub revues and a few framed photographs of long-faded European stars decorate the walls. A typewriter clacks from an inner office.

The typing ceases and a man comes out. He is thickset, maybe fifty. His black hair is slicked back in comb-marked waves; a thin wisp of a mustache dusts his upper lip; thick glasses magnify huge, swimming eyeballs.

"Bonjour," I begin. "Je suis Rebecca Bell, une chanteuse Américaine. Chris Fargate…" I've run out of French. "He gave me your name and said you represented singers. I have, I mean, j'ai…" *What the hell is the word for tapes?* I pull the demo tape out of my bag and hand it to him. "Je voudrais chanter a Paris." I would like to sing in Paris, I hope I said.

"Comment?"

"Bonjour. Je suis Rebecca Bell, une chanteuse américaine, et—"

"Yes, I hear all of zat."

He speaks English like Inspector Clouseau. His feet splay like a duck. It's all I can do not to laugh at this preposterous man.

"Chris Fargate said you book clubs and cafes."

His eyebrows are thin and dyed black. "Yes. He call me about you. So…you are singair? There are sousands of singairs, sousands of pretty girls. Why I should listen to you?"

"Well, because…" I've never been very good at touting my own talents. "Because I'm good?"

He gives an impatient shrug and leads the way into his office, where he places my tape on an ancient recorder, carefully winding it around the reel. My voice leaps out, too loud. The tapes were recorded in a friend's living room and they sound it. Armand Frochot closes his eyes, listening. After the second song, he snaps it off. "You have nice voice. But vairee high. Can you sing lowair? We French prefer Piaf, not so much Joan Baez."

"Yes. Oui. Of course."

"You are lucky today. I know a club that can use za girl singair. Many Americans go there. Très élégante."

"That sounds wonderful! And I sing in French, too." Well, I know three French songs. "Where is the club?"

"Abidjan."

At my blank look, he explains, "The capital city of Ivory Coast in Afrique. The Diamond International Hotel. Beautiful nightclub, beautiful city, many tourists with a lot of money."

"But I just got here. I want to work in Paris."

He waves his hand impatiently. "Of course, of course," he says, "I know many bookings. But they pay very little. No money, what is the point?"

"Well, I guess I'd like to be here more than a week."

"There is a hotel in Marseilles, très belle. That is in France. Ees near the Riviera. Many rich men."

"I'm sure there are, but I want to stay in Paris, for a while anyway."

"You are stubborn, you are determined to be poor. D'accord, I know a place, they will like you. Is a bar, nothing fancy, but many clientele anglaise. Can you sing tonight? Audition, no pay."

"Oui."

"Bon. Dress in something ravissant. And don' zeeng so high."

Le Scorpion, on the Boulevard des Capucines, turns out to be a B-movie version of the American Old West. The pub is below street level, down a creaky flight of stairs. I cross an overpass that looks down on another floor to the bar and the main room. It's like the whole place started as a bomb shelter, with descending levels. Patrons, beer steins in hand, lean over the railing watching the smoke-swathed swarms of post-happy hour humanity below. Noise bangs against the unbattened walls. I can see a small stage with a battered upright piano and a microphone stand.

I continue down the stairs, lifting the hem of my long coat with one hand while grasping the guitar case in the other. The walls are adorned with old harness equipment, pictures of cowboys, and "Wanted: Dead or Alive" posters. On the bar level, a thick layer of sawdust coats the floor. There's an entryway to a back room. Inside, a smaller bar is unattended, and there are a few tiny tables and a mike in the far corner. When I re-emerge into the main area, I'm face to face with Armand Frochot.

"Ah, bon, you are here! Wait, I bring l'impresario." The jukebox blasts "Hey, Jude," several of the customers lustily singing along. Frochot returns with a short and stocky guy stuffed into a Western-cut suit. Eduard "Eddy" Michel, proprietor of the Scorpion. The two men converse loud and fast in French. I surmise from the way they're pointing at the front bar and then at the empty back room that there has been some misunderstanding about where I'm to perform.

I take off my coat. The male attention swivels in my direction. I'm wearing the black, backless, décolleté dress that shows my body to great advantage but looks startlingly out of place in a funky pub. It's the dress I was wearing the night I met Harry, purchased for three dollars in a thrift shop. Who was the rich woman who cast this off?

"C'est magnifique!" the pub manager exclaims.

I unpack the guitar and attempt to tune up, while the jukebox pumps out "Rocket Man." Michel makes a throat-slicing motion to the bartender. The music cuts off. A few customers grumble and watch indifferently as M. Michel climbs onto the stage and yells into the microphone. "Un, deux, trois, bonsoir, 'sieurs, dames, bienvenue!"

There must be a place in the universe where club managers are spawned from one huge coarse egg.

"... chanteuse Américaine!"

The male patrons shout and whistle. I've already discarded the set of sensitive ballads, which I'd planned for a reverent, darkened room, with bereted Frenchmen sipping wine and sighing in romantic transport. I can barely hear myself. Frochot and Michel are huddled in an animated conversation. Sweat drips down my sides.

"Hey, sweetie!" a patron yells in Brit English. "How about 'I Can't Get No Satisfaction'?" He sidles up to the stage and touches my ankle. I kick his hand. The men near him give a whoop of appreciation.

The whole thing reminds me of my short-lived stint as a go-go dancer at the Peacock Lounge in Hackensack, New Jersey. This was during one of my more desperate periods before *Au Naturel!* when gigs were few and far between and the only other option was office temping.

Go-Girl Entertainments was in a ramshackle, six-story building on West 56th Street, just off Eighth Avenue. Two agents, Gus and Jerry, ran it. Gus did most of the talking, while Jerry stared at me and sucked on a cigar.

"You ever dance before? Professionally?" Gus appeared to be the leader.

"I was in a musical and there was dancing."

They shared a look.

"You want to dance topless or with a top?" Gus continued.

"A top."

Jerry mashed his cigar tip into a brimming ashtray.

"So." Gus squinted. "You wanna audition? You know. Dance around?"

If I turned sharply left, I could injure myself on a wooden swivel chair. To the right: a desk piled high with glossy photos. An ancient coffee maker teetered on the edge of the desk. "There's no music."

"That's okay. Jerry'll sing."

Jerry launched into an a capella version of "I Heard It Through the Grapevine." I moved around in the tiny space, at one point accidentally knocking over a stack of magazines. "Sorry."

"Don't worry," Gus pushed the debris out of the way with his foot. "You're good."

"Good-looking, too." Jerry's voice was rusty, as if rarely used.

"You need something that sparkles under the light." Gus handed me a business card. "Down on 46th, they sell go-go stuff, G-strings, stripper gizmos. Tell 'em you're from Go-Girl Entertainment and they'll give you a discount."

"I'm not going to wear a G-string."

"No, 'course not! We run a classy organization. Get the go-go two-piece."

"We gotta name her."

"My name's Rebecca."

"We name all our girls," Gus explained. "What if we had two Rebeccas? It could get confusing."

Jerry piped up. "Rose Red? Like in that fairy tale my kid likes."

Gus loved this. "Check the calendar."

Jerry slowly leafed through the big ledger. Impatient, Gus grabbed it and stuck his finger onto an empty square on the page. "We got the Peacock Lounge in Hackensack tonight. Mustang Sally cancelled."

Gus explained what bus to take from the Port Authority Bus Terminal. "You'll dance twenty minutes on, twenty off, till one. We'll pick you up after, get you back to the city. Pay is thirty-five, cash. Don't

worry about our cut, we collect from the clubs at the end of the week."
He puts out his hand. "Welcome to our stable."

That night a blue and red neon bird flashed over the Peacock
Lounge, with a large-lettered sign underneath: "Direct from New York!
Live Go-Go Girls!" Inside, my eyes adjusted to the dim light. A long bar
on the right, with a mirror behind it, the walls papered in red velveteen.
A few tables with fat candle jars wrapped in netted plastic. At the end
of the room, a pink spotlight and a black light for psychedelic effect
illuminated a small, raised platform. Christmas decorations on the
walls; angels, silver bells, and tinsel looped over the bar's mirror, in late
February. A large fish tank behind the bar revealed a puffy, scowling
piranha. A middle-aged man in a seasoned leather jacket nursed a beer.
The bartender, thickset and impassive, washed a soapy glass.

"I'm Rebecca, I mean Rose, the dancer for tonight."

"Change in the ladies room. Back there." He indicated with his head.

The one-bowl room was dark and reeked of Airwick. I changed as
quickly as possible, bare feet on a cold linoleum floor as I wrestled into
pantyhose. The bottom half of the thirty-dollar, two-piece costume was
a scantily cut bikini, woven with gold and silver beading in the design of
a butterfly. The top, a sparkly, fringed push-up bra that lifted my breasts
as if they were on a platter.

Can things get worse than this?

"Leave your stuff in the kitchen," the bartender told me when I slunk
out, the costume partially covered by a long cardigan. He handed me
three quarters. "Five songs. That's just about twenty minutes. What's
your name again?"

"Reb...uh, Rose Red."

"We've had a Pepper, a Lightning, a Cinnamon, a Chiclets. They
wanted to send us a *Licorice* and I had to tell 'em, no, this bar ain't a
'licorice' kinda crowd, if you get my meaning."

I dropped the quarters in the jukebox, scanning the song titles for
what might be good ones to dance to. A James Brown tune, the Eagles'

"Witchy Woman," something called "Jungle Fever," and two Rolling Stones; "I Can't Get No Satisfaction" and "Jumpin' Jack Flash."

For the first few songs, I was hopelessly awkward and stiff, just moving around, turning, kicking, flapping my arms. I could do this a lot better in a crowded discotheque. More male customers came in, and watched without expression. I ramped it up for "Satisfaction." The piranha swam circles in its tank. I turned and turned. Ceiling, floor, bar, fish. Guy at bar: "Smile, honey." *Fuck you.*

Now, at Le Scorpion in Paris, I am beginning to appreciate the relative serenity of the Peacock Lounge in Hackensack. A beer bottle crashes to the floor, spraying liquid. The crowd cheers, as drunks do when glass breaks. Fuck it. If they aren't going to shut up, I might as well get them all singing along. I go into "Those Were the Days," and the Brits happily join in the chorus.

A bouncer heaves the bottle thrower up the stairs and out the door.

The audience is with me now and they yell for more when I finish my three songs and clamber down from the stage.

"He loves you!" Frochot shouts, nodding toward the club owner.

"Are you kidding me? This is a fucking zoo. How do you say *that* in French? Comment dites-vous 'fucking zoo'?"

"'Un zoo foutou,'" he offers, helpfully. "But he pay you one hundred francs! In dollars, that ees…"

"I don't give a crap. I'd rather sing in the street."

I spot a familiar profile on the upper level. *No, it can't be.* He's heading to the exit. I push my way across the room and up the stairs and out the door into the street.

It's middle-of-the-night cold, desolate, newspaper-blowing empty. I see the man getting into a cab. He turns back for a moment, as if he's forgotten something. It's not Harry. Doesn't even look like him. A car passes, slows, two men lean out, yell a few foul French words, then rev on. A dog barks in the distance.

Is this the way it's going to be? Chasing ghosts in the middle of the night?

"Where do you run to?" Frochot demands when I return, out of breath and freezing.

"I thought I saw someone I knew."

"So, you do not want to sing here. Je comprends. C'est 'un zoo foutou.'" He places my coat over my bare shoulders. "Come, ma chèrie. I take you to Les Halles, we have soupe à l'oignon. You have seen Les Halles? The covered marketplace? No? Well, better not to wait, they are tearing it down every day. Most of it is gone. I will tell you about my other ideas for you."

Only a few years before, President Charles de Gaulle had ordered the old Halles market demolished and moved to a distant suburb. Paris' largest wholesale fruit and vegetable and fish district has been ripped out of the heart of the Right Bank, leaving a huge, gaping construction site the Parisians derisively refer to as *le trou*, the hole.

One day, the developers promise, there will be new buildings, a museum, an underground mall, a Metro line. But for now, the blocks of shabby, fragrant, teeming stalls where for centuries Parisians gathered to shop for fresh food, are all but gone. A few restaurants and stalls remain, clinging to the Old World in the face of imminent demolition, and a few new eateries have optimistically opened.

When we're seated at a cozy booth at L'Escargot Montorgueil, one of the historic holdouts, Frochot orders two soups and a plate of fresh oysters. He is sentimental, almost weeping, as he describes the culinary joys of the old Les Halles. Émile Zola, he says, once described the district as "le ventre de Paris" – the belly of Paris. Since the early twelfth century, the sprawling food market defined the area and received a much-needed restoration in the 1850s, with the construction of large iron-and-glass pavilions to shelter the vendors' stalls.

"That," Frochot says with some scorn, waving his arm toward *le trou*, "is catastrophe. *Le monstre* architecture, big and ugly for our city, like the towers they are building in your New York."

I'd only seen the new downtown towers from a distance, rising like two upended rows of staples, unbalancing the skyline, as if the narrow island of Manhattan might tip over from their excess weight.

He gives a cynical, Gallic shrug. "But the world must move forward."

The soup arrives, steaming under thick, melting Gruyere. The oysters are perfect, sea-tanged globules, at once luscious and alien. We wash them down with chilled Sancerre.

"But let us talk about you, Rebecca. I can see you are vairy sensitive artiste. The Scorpion bar ees not the place for someone like you. You are vairy special woman…"

Oh, Lord, here it comes…

"And eef woman is what I like, for romance…mais non, I prefer zee man."

Thank god.

"So," Frochot continues, "You do not like to go to Abidjan, too many black Africans…"

"It's not the *black* people."

"You will make money, then you come back to Paris. I will find you a recording contract! There are many wonderful places: Luanda. Marrakesh. Tehran. Beirut…"

"Wait. Tehran? Iran?"

"Iran, Persia, yes. This ees *vairy* special, very high class. The most luxury of the Diamond Hotels. The best." He kisses his fingers.

"Maybe. Let me think about it."

10

"Tehran?" Max snakes his way to the front of the cafeteria line at the Alliance Française. I already have a plate of aromatic beef chasseur and a small bottle of red table wine (three francs extra) on my tray. He continues talking as we go to the table he saved with his jacket and books as markers. "You don't know anyone there, you don't speak the language – what *is* the language?"

"Persian?"

"What if something happens to you?"

"I didn't say I'd go. Yet. This agent wants to send me to the far corners."

"This is the same genius who thought the Scorpion was a good idea, right?"

"He also mentioned Abidjan. That's the Ivory Coast. Oh, and Luanda."

"I need an atlas."

"It's in Angola. 'The Paris of Africa,' he tells me."

"How about the Paris of Paris?"

"And Marrakesh."

"Is the club called Rick's?" Max grabs a handful of napkins from another table. "You've barely gotten here. If you need a loan…"

47

"No, it isn't the money. Well, it *is* a lot of money. And the Diamond Hotels are fabulous. There's one in New York, it's one of the best places. Hey, I know first-hand, I've used their lobby ladies room!" I don't add that I once spent a night in a Diamond Hotel penthouse with Harry. "And it isn't like I'll never be back. It's just a month or two." I start to pour a glass of wine, spill it, and quickly sop it up with a paper napkin.

Max busies himself twisting a straw into knots. "Sounds like you've already decided."

"I guess I have."

"Tehran is supposed to be beautiful. Very cosmopolitan, royal family and all."

"If they don't like me, I'll be back on the next plane."

"Of course they'll like you. How could they not? You're beautiful, you're brilliant…"

"You're nuts."

"That, too." He waggles his eyebrows like Groucho Marx. Max is the nice sort of guy I ought to love.

"I'm not sure I'll fit in. I'm a folksinger, not some glossy nightclub act."

"Why would he send you all that way if he didn't think you'd fit? Oh, wait. The Scorpion." He pushes his food around on the plate. "Won't you be lonely?"

"I'm lonely here." I add, quickly, "I mean, until I met you."

He puts his hand over mine. "Please, don't do that bullshit with me."

"What bullshit?"

"The seductive, eyelash-fluttering thing you do with men."

"Fuck you."

"That's more like it." He tosses back his wine. "I just want you to be careful. If you need anything, or just want to talk, call me. Please. Call collect if you have to. Call me even if you don't want to talk. I can always think of a joke." He adds, "Farsi."

"Is that a punch line?"

"No. That's what they speak in Iran."

In the morning, I stop by Frochot's office to discuss the job and the travel arrangements – I'll be leaving in less than a week – but I can barely absorb the mundane details. And what if Harry is still here in Paris and I've missed him? But Fargate hinted that Harry had dealings in Iran. And fuck Harry anyway. Maybe he can start looking for *me*. It makes no sense, but I really don't think Harry is in Paris.

This beautiful city has barely felt my footsteps. I want to leave some imprint, like a trail of invisible crumbs, so that I can find my way back one day.

The Rodin Museum is only a few Metro stops away at Varenne. I'll be a tourist. I'll buy crepes from a street vendor, stop for coffee in a working-class *café-tabac*. Pretend I'm an existentialist en route to meet my lover, Jean-Paul Sartre. I will embrace every cliché from every American-in-Paris movie. Perhaps I'll even *go* to the movies, and see *Last Tango in Paris*.

The city is dressed for Christmas; the *buche de noel* cakes in the windows of the patisseries, the lights along the Champs Élysée from Concorde to Étoile. A giant red ribbon adorns the Arc de Triomphe. What a fool I am to miss this! I'll tell Frochot I changed my mind.

But the Paris of my dreams was Harry; without him, it's just another town. And there's the money. And the possibility, however slim, that Harry's in Iran.

11

Chris Fargate lives in a spacious apartment on the top floor of a large private home, near the Bois de Boulogne.

"Becky, you look wonderful!" He kisses me on both cheeks. "Paris will miss you and I will be bereft." He hands me a snifter of brandy. "Although it will be fascinating where you're going. An amazing part of the world." He straightens a picture on the wall. "Please, have a seat." An antique sofa of some French king vintage. "I have a small favor to ask."

"Okay…"

"You were such a dear to bring Alistair's gift *all* the way from London."

He makes it sound as if I towed a car across the Channel.

"And now I need to send that very same item on another leg of its journey."

Chris opens a locked cabinet and takes out a familiar box. The brown paper wrapping is loosened, the string untied. "We need to get Alistair's little artifact into Iran."

"I could take it to the post office and mail it."

"Well, you did slip our little friend past customs once without so much as a why or wherefore." He chuckles. "Frankly—"

Whenever someone starts a sentence with "frankly" you just know you don't want to hear the rest.

"—it all comes down to money and I'm as cheap as they come. The tariffs are high, and there *is* some question of the provenance. The piece has had a series of owners who, shall we say, didn't keep the best records. If I mail it, I'll have to insure it, and deal with even more red tape and bureaucracy. So you see, it's easier to have someone carry it through."

"Is it valuable?"

"Not especially. Zand Bahador was a Persian sculptor who had a brief popularity in Tehran in the twenties. There was some kind of political scandal and he fell out of favor. There are actually only a few remaining examples of his work."

"They must be worth *some*thing."

"Not so much now. But I think they have some potential to appreciate. There's some…uh…political unrest that has revived Bahador's reputation as a kind of rebel. Don't worry, nothing dangerous over there, just a few troublemakers who don't like the Shah. Art investing can be like playing the stock market." He rummages in a drawer, takes out a Xeroxed article, and hands it to me.

According to the article, printed in a European arts magazine dated March 1966, a number of Iranian artists had their works stolen. A British couple became patrons of the arts in Tehran in the 1950s and '60s and specialized in finding artists whose work had been obscure or suppressed for political reasons. One of the artists, unnamed, whose work was in the "Lost Collection," told the reporter, "The collectors were living in Tehran and asked a number of artists to give them art to sell in the new gallery they were opening in London. I gave five paintings, others gave many more, and some came from family collections. There were a lot of promises but we were never paid, and just recently we saw some of the works listed in a Christie's sale. We tried to negotiate with Christie's but the terms were unacceptable." Fearing bad publicity and a lawsuit, Christie's cancelled the sale and returned the works to the British collectors.

The article goes on to list the artists whose works disappeared. One is Zand Bahador, who died in 1926.

The door blows open as if a ghost has burst through it. No one is there. Fargate closes it. "Crazy wind," he says. He tightens the wrapping around the statuette and knots the string. "The Diamond International is a wonderful opportunity. Frochot is working on some recording deals for you, and when you come back, you'll have plenty to live on while you start your first record and build your continental career. Just enjoy the whole adventure, meet people, gather memories. Perhaps you'll snag a royal and become another Princess Grace."

"I suppose you'll be paying me a courier fee. Like Alistair did."

He looks startled but opens the top desk drawer and rummages around. "Yes, yes, of course."

The phone rings. Fargate picks it up and talks rapidly in French, too fast for me to catch more than a few words. But one of these is "agneau." This is a word I happen to know because of a French Christmas carol that contains the phrase; *Le précieux Agneau de Dieu.*" The precious *lamb* of God.

I can't think of a good reason why Christopher Fargate would be talking about the "Lamb of God." But I can think of a man named Harry Lamb.

Is someone else looking for Harry? A shiver of anticipation, a mix of fear and excitement is so intense, I nearly lose my balance.

Chris hangs up the phone. "Are you all right?"

"Yes. Fine. I forgot to have breakfast, I guess."

"Can I get you something? A cup of tea?"

"Can't stay. Just the…fee would be good."

He puts a wad of cash in an envelope and hands it over with the package.

"What do I do with it when I get there?"

"Don't worry, a dealer friend of mine will contact you. Bon voyage, sweetie."

12

I join my small group of short-lived acquaintances at a café off Avenue Rapp for a bon voyage party. Max gives me a *Speak Farsi!* paperback he picked up at a second-hand bookstore.

Ellen returns from the ladies room, informing us, with a shudder, "One of those 'hole in the floor hang onto the handles' *horrors*."

"Well, here's to Rebecca's great adventure! May the Diamond Hotel have fabulous bathrooms." Max raises his glass. "*L'chaim.*"

Ellen snorts, "Better not say that *there*. Too *Jewish*." She takes the last of the frites from Jimmy's plate.

"Well, I'm not Jewish. Unless Pentecostals are one of the Lost Tribes of Israel."

Max signals the waiter for the check. "Seems like there're more Lost Tribes than original ones." He touches my hand. "Iran is a very civilized country. The Shah and his family are elegant and Westernized. He also has a nice big army and lots of SAVAK policemen to keep the rabble from killing him. And fortunately, our wonderful government is sending him F-14s and missiles and bombs in case things get out of hand."

"That's certainly reassuring." I reach for the check to see what my share is but Max shakes his head.

Ellen turns to me. "Your family, they were Pentecostals? Speaking in tongues and all of that?"

"The Jesus of the Spirit Pentecostal Union of God. My dad was a minister. My mother did hands-on healing."

"For real?"

"Oh, very real. At least they believed it, and so did the congregation. I think they did help a lot of people, although whether it's power of suggestion or some kind of miracle...who knows?"

"Where's your family now?" Ellen asks.

"They died. A car accident." I say it like they'd moved to Florida. It's never seemed quite real to me, more like something I saw on a TV show a long time ago.

Max stares at me, concern in his eyes. "I'm so sorry."

I want to brush his words away like the graveyard dust that rose in spirals on the windy day they were all buried. I had a scarf around my face, with a cat design. Whatever happened to that scarf? So many things fall away.

A record is playing, or is it the radio?

"La neige tombe sur la mer...les oiseaux-lyres ont oublié comment chanter..."

Is it still snowing on the sea? Have I forgotten how to sing, like the lyrebirds?

Max brings me back to the present. "It must have been hard to leave the people you knew, the life you knew, and make such a big change, going to New York and everything." He refills our glasses with the remaining house red wine. "Sorry, I'm too nosy."

"No, no, not at all." The memories are a shroud I can't shrug off. Outside the window of the café, Parisian nightlife bustles. As in New York, everyone is in a hurry.

I always knew I would leave the Midwest. New York had not been my first choice. I had vague dreams of Hollywood, until I met a New Yorker. This was in Missouri, and about as common a sighting as finding a two-headed snake. Mrs. Lamire was a high school English teacher, and a transplant to the Midwest with her husband, a native of St. Louis. I had been outed as "home schooled" by a police officer who wondered why I wasn't in school in the middle of the day, and was unimpressed by my explanation. He contacted my parents and insisted I get registered for a real education.

Mrs. Lamire was in her late thirties, a short, stocky woman with a brash energy and a passion for literature. We were assigned – and I devoured – a wide range of nineteenth and twentieth-century novels. *The Great Gatsby. The Catcher in the Rye* – until it was put on a banned list, *Tess of the D'Urbervilles* – until my mother discovered that it had the shocking plot about a young woman who gets pregnant out of wedlock.

Mrs. Lamire talked about the New York Public Library, with its great stone lions flanking the entrance, and the vast walls lined with books. She made literature come to life; poor Tess, wandering the countryside of the fictional Wessex; Holden, whose intimate knowledge of Manhattan astonished me. Mrs. Lamire told me I was smart, and not just another female biding her time till marriage. I wasn't sure I wanted to be smart because the smart girls were considered to be full of themselves or dowdy or arrogant – meaning they didn't let the man feel superior. And they were poor candidates for wife and motherhood. Young Christian women were supposed to be deferential – to father, to pastor (in my case one and the same), and most of all, to God.

Mrs. Lamire left at the end of the school year. I wondered if she'd gone back to New York City, and when I got there a few years later, I kept hoping that somehow I'd run into her.

In a flurry of goodbyes, I leave Max, Ellen, and Jimmy at the café, and within moments they have vanished from my mind, replaced by new distractions and plans, the slant of evening light, the pinch of my left boot, the desire for a shower. I pause in front of a bookshop, considering whether to buy a book to read on the plane. A reflection appears in the shop window, a man's form that tugs at the corners of my recent memory. I noticed him, but as a background player. He wears a brown corduroy jacket that looks as if it had been buried in a secondhand bin for months.

He passes me, turns and stops. "The little snake. It's mine." His body is poised to run – or pounce. Is he making a sexual suggestion? What man would say "little"? He pulls back his jacket, revealing the glint of a knife. I trip backwards. The streets are crowded with people on their way home from work. A gun would be reassuring right at this moment. My father taught my brother and me to shoot when we were growing up. He said even a woman should know how to defend herself. *Especially* a woman. But I don't have a gun.

"Fuck off. I'll call the police. *Les flics.*"

"Not always *les flics* around," he says, turning quickly and disappearing down the steps of the Metro.

The fear hits after the fact. I almost sink to the ground in a faint, like some Victorian lady in a too-tight corset. There's a *café-tabac* nearby with a phone in the back. I drop a token into the box and dial Chris's home. It rings and rings. No one answers at the gallery, either.

I should go to the American Consulate. The police. I should buy a ticket back to New York with Chris Fargate's money. I should return to my hotel, get the statuette, and dump it in the Seine.

I don't do any of those things. My brain swirls with biblical images and sounds.

God's grace is open to all who "confess with their mouth," the Holy Ghost will enter the believer, "fill" the "clean vessel," and he or I will immediately speak in tongues…

Exhorters, members of the congregation who have already had tongues – cluster around the seekers and help pray them through. The seekers pray themselves into trance…

> *kantášabaravo sántolavo.*
> *ílamašax rábaxo kalarábou.*
> *rišádalabo píta rabása tóyen …*

Bowl of Night

I walk aimlessly, unaware of where I'm going, until I recognize the vast, manicured gardens of Champ de Mars, the Eiffel Tower in the distance. Up in the restaurant on the top level, people are dining in that aerie, beautifully dressed, in the midst of their romantic trysts. (Although they are more likely to be tired and cranky from relentless sightseeing, arguing over who messed up the directions, and whether in the morning they should join the masses staring at the Mona Lisa or take the bus tour to Versailles.)

The elevator is crowded, a babble of languages. Up we go, the ground shrinking, the lights below spreading out and out, ocean of light, city of light, blending into the stars, and the GermanFrenchItalianEnglishJapanese people enthralled.

I am here, and there is this moment.

Tears fall down my cheeks. I hide behind my hair. The elevator reaches the pinnacle of the Tower of Babel, and I step out into muted luxuries, recalling that Chris Fargate said the food is not good here, it just appeals to the tourists. His words echo in my head. *Just enjoy the whole adventure, meet people, gather memories. Perhaps you'll snag a royal and become another Princess Grace.*

The vast window reveals all of Paris, glittering in the night. I step out onto the lookout, the wind whipping up. I have the sensation of falling, my legs going all shivery as if the body is at the mercy of the mind and it might decide to fly away. The Seine, leaden cold and pockmarked with rain, appears alarmingly close, as if it were reaching up.

Part II

13

The KLM 747 floats onto the tarmac at Tehran Mehrabad airport at seven-thirty in the morning. The flight began in Paris the previous afternoon, with a long layover in Amsterdam. As soon as the plane rolls to a halt, I stand, stooping under the luggage holder like giant Alice in the White Rabbit's house. My seatmate is a husky man in a white Muslim cap; he never so much as glanced at me during the entire trip and took pains not to brush against me in any way. I wish I'd been seated farther back, with the boisterous backpacking Dutch and German students.

While waiting in the customs line, I study Max's English-Farsi translation book, seeking out useful phrases: *Namifahmam* (I don't understand); *Raheh Konsoolgari-ye-ambooerika kojast?* (Which is the way to the American Consulate?); *Keili garan aft* (It's too expensive.) A man behind me holds a plastic portable radio and listens to news delivered in fast, staccato Arabic. I pick up words here and there: Israel. Arafat. Black September. The news ends and music takes its place, a jumble of bouncing rhythms, quavering strings, and a high-voiced singer moaning some profound, undulating pain. The music is compelling, but it would be nice if the singer picked one note and stuck with it for a few bars.

Bowl of Night

The line through customs moves quickly, overseen by men in military uniforms. A customs agent asks if I'm carrying more than the allotted 200 cigarettes. I tell him I don't smoke, and he is happy to take my word for it.

In the ladies room, a businesswoman in a crisp gray suit smiles at me in the mirror as we wash our hands side by side. "American?" she asks. "Your first time here? It's a beautiful country. But complicated."

The airport encompasses a medley of dress and cultures. Young travelers in the universal Western denim; a statuesque African couple, their blue-black skin offset by bright, multi-colored robes; an emaciated, turbaned beggar. As I drag my luggage toward the exit, I see a man in Arab headdress and robes, trailed by four women, all of whom are shrouded in black *burqas*. Their eyes are like those of trapped animals inside a mesh cage. Yet the airport is as undeniably modern as any other international arrivals terminal in the States. What did I expect? Camels? A big, sandy Arabia? There's comfort in the urban familiarity.

Dozens of small orange taxis crowd the airport entrance. A driver grabs my bag, commenting on the guitar as he tosses it into the trunk, all the while smiling and pretending not to look at my body. I tug my coat closed, covering low-slung jeans and a close-fitting black V-necked sweater. As we pull away from the curb, I notice four military men lounging at the entrance to the airport, laughing and smoking, army rifles slung casually at their sides.

The taxi eases into traffic and then onto a fast, windy highway. Dust spirals dance along the roadside. The snow-capped peaks of the Elburz mountain chain are visible in the north, the Caspian Sea is beyond the mountains, and past that the U.S.S.R. Cars race and swerve around one another as if this were the Indianapolis Speedway. It's even worse as we enter the city; traffic crams the streets, cars and trucks fighting for space with motorcycles, the ubiquitous orange taxis, and an occasional donkey cart. Many streets and buildings and stores are called Pahlavi and Reza and Shah, or some combination of the royal family names.

The cab rolls up a curved driveway, spewing white dust. Monsieur Frochot had not lied when he described the hotel as deluxe, yet I hadn't imagined its palatial dimensions and imposing gaudiness. Tall, pink-marble columns flank wide front doors, gilded with mosaic. The hotel name is revealed on a discreet copper plaque:

The Diamond International Hotel of Tehran.
سامل‌ا ى‌ل‌ل‌مل‌ا ن‌ى‌ب ل‌ت‌ه

A bellboy in a white uniform takes my bags and whisks them through the vast lobby to the front desk. The desk clerk regards me with real interest and says, in clear, accented English, "You are the famous American singer! We are so pleased to have you!"

Perhaps they have me mixed up with some other singer? More likely, Frochot sold them a convincing line of bullshit. After registering, I follow the bellboy to the elevator, which is only slightly less ornamented than an illustration in the *Arabian Nights*, and up to the eighth floor to my suite. Now I'm certain they've taken me for someone else. The spacious sitting room has gleaming tile floors, partially covered by a plush Persian carpet. Wide double windows open onto a patio with a view of the mountains.

"Pretty, yes?" the bellboy says. "The cousin of the Shabanou stay here. And also the Godfather, Marlon Brando."

The adjoining bedroom, twice as big as my entire apartment back in New York, is decorated in white and coral, and a smaller Persian carpet accents the foot of the bed, which is covered in a soft, gold-tasseled spread. The bathroom features sparkling mirror glass mosaics; a giant tub and separate shower; a marble hand basin with gold, swan-shaped spigots, and a bidet. The toilet has its own little closet.

I want to fall to the ground in gratitude.

The bellboy places my suitcase on a stand. I thrust a combination of French and British bills into his hand. When he's gone, I check that the door is locked, and experience full quiet for the first time in days. The plane engine still rings in my ears. The hotel is sufficiently set back from the wide Boulevard Karim Khan-Izand to render the traffic noise a dim and distant hum, occasionally punctuated by car horns.

The desk clerk has told me that the hotel is within walking distance of many interesting and scenic places, such as the university and Farah Park, but I would probably want to take a taxi to Golestan Palace and The King's Mosque, to see the crown jewels, which are kept in a bank vault. He mentioned the fabulous bazaars in the south of the city. All I want now is a bath and a nap.

I open the windows wide, breathing in the cold air. The blue-sky view is as picturesque as a tourist postcard. A handful of white fluff clouds surround the perfect, snow-capped peak of Mount Damavand.

Monsieur Frochot gave me the name of the entertainment director, Mohammed Meskat, but no number or extension, and I'm too tired to care. Besides, when they realize I'm not famous or important, they'll probably move me to a maid's room or ship me back to Paris.

14

The phone rings in short jabs, waking me from a jetlagged coma. I'm unsure of the day, the year, the country.

"Mademoiselle Bell?" a man asks. "I am Meskat. I am in charge of the musical entertainment." He wants to meet me in the lobby when I am "refreshed."

The room is dark, save for a stream of streetlight that casts shadows on the bed. It is also freezing. I wrap myself in the bedspread, close the window, and search for a heat source. There is a control box on the wall with red and blue symbols that suggested hot and cold. I push red, and a few moments later, heat steams up through pipes that sound a lot like the ones in my Manhattan tenement.

When the elevator doors open in the lobby, a man steps forward and grasps my hand in a formal shake. "Yes, you are just like your photograph, Miss Bell! We are very happy you came all this way to perform for our guests. A Broadway star!"

Meskat is shorter than me, with a hooked nose and a thin, worried mouth that works hard to smile. "Follow me." He opens a double door to a wide hallway. We pass a banquet hall, in the midst of being set up for a party, a conference room, rows of shops and boutiques, and at the end of the long corridor, a nightclub.

"This is our Scheherazade Room," Meskat says proudly,

A standing sign features glossy photographs of the performers. I recognize the one I gave Frochot in Paris, a moody view taken last year, pre-Harry, by a photographer boyfriend —well, "boyfriend" is a bit of a euphemism—of "girl and guitar," as he called it. The photo session had culminated in a roll of soft-focus nude shots and a roll in the hay.

Next to my picture is one of a mature woman bursting out of a sequined dress, and another shows a rotund, smiling Arab man brandishing a balloon animal. A sign invites the audience to "Dance at the Diamond Discothèque!"

The club is huge, with at least a hundred tables. Behind a long bar, two bartenders slice lemons and limes and crush ice with mallets. I have never played in a club this size.

"This is not satisfactory for your talents?" Meskat frowns, catching my expression. "It is one of Tehran's best nightclubs!" He has to raise his voice over the din of the ice crushing.

I had envisioned a cozy supper club or intimate lounge. "I can see that, but the thing is, I like to be close to the audience, because it's just me and my guitar, and I tend to sing quiet songs."

"That is no problem," he says, pleased to have an easy solution. "We have many loud microphones! Everyone will hear you!" He fusses with one of the tablecloths, picks up a wine glass, and holds it to the light, clearly unhappy. "Hamou!" he barks. A waiter scurries over. Meskat speaks quickly in Farsi, and the offending glass is taken away. He returns to me. "We have other performers, of course. Valerie Marchand, the French star." He says the name with some awe. "And our own funny comedian, Omar Khash. The Scheherazade Orchestra is finest in the city! Please to let me know anything you might need. The show starts at nine o'clock. First Omar will warm up the audience with his comedy jokes, then you will sing, and then our lovely Valerie Marchand. She has been here for two years, you know," he confides. "Very very popular. But you will be popular, too, and maybe stay even longer."

I want to suggest that two female singers in a row is probably not the best running order. But Valerie Marchand's music is sure to be quite different from mine.

"Oh, I nearly forget!" Meskat says. "Of course, you must see the dressing rooms! We will go from the front, but you will come in later from the side hall." I follow him up the low steps to the stage, making my way gingerly over tangles of electrical cords and music stands and band chairs, through a tasseled side curtain and into a short, dark corridor. The second door is my dressing room, a bright, comfortable space with a sofa, lighted mirror and small table. Flowers bloom in a mosaic vase.

Meskat says I'm welcome to have dinner in the main dining room before the show – complimentary, of course. He leaves to attend to his other duties.

I head back through the lobby. Music is playing, quietly.

"...*La neige tombe sur la mer ... C'est la fin de l'affaire...*"

15

he contents of my suitcase resemble the wreckage of an air disaster. I do my makeup and hair several times, trying to determine just what says "sophisticated nightclub" yet still suggests "earthy folk roots." At past nine o'clock, the show is starting. I rush from the elevator, take a wrong turn into a private dinner party, then into a storage room, and finally down another hall, startling two men in tuxes sharing a hash pipe. "Where is backstage?" I ask. One of the men points at a door a few feet away. It leads to a short hallway, and the back of the bandstand. There are bursts of laughter from the audience, and the staccato rhythms of a comedian. Meskat appears out of the shadows.

"Are you finding your dressing room?" He looks up and down the length of me. I'm not sure if he's impressed or appalled. My dress is the same skin-bearing one I had worn to the abysmal audition at Le Scorpion in Paris. He raises an eyebrow and gives an approximation of a smile, so I take that to mean he likes it.

Meskat escorts me to my dressing room once again. There is a bouquet of flowers in a cut glass vase, and a small card with my name. It isn't easy to misspell Rebecca, but someone has managed it: Rebeka Bell. Still, it is a sweet gesture. Meskat, who likely wrote the card, and is standing in the doorway, beams at me. 'I will let you prepare." With a little bow, he goes out, leaving the door open.

I carefully tune my guitar. If only I had thought to change the strings! If only I had better material, more French songs, an Iranian song! I copy the set onto a small piece of paper and tape it to the top of the guitar.

There's a soft knock and a beautiful woman sweeps into the room in a waft of perfume. I recognize Valerie Marchand from her photo, at the same time realizing just how old a photo it is. Nevertheless, the bone structure goddess has greatly blessed Madame Marchand, who is poured into a green satin dress, hair a bottle red-orange, hard and puffy, her eyelids thick with glitter. Despite all the brass, she has an alluring, seasoned sensuality.

"So you're the folksinger," she purrs. "Monsieur Meskat, he is such a character in a bad play, no? But sweet." Valerie meanders around my dressing room, idly rummaging through my things. "This is nice room, *très belle*, but small." Apparently satisfied that she has the better dressing room, Valerie wishes me a good show, with the traditional French expletive, "Merde!" and leaves.

Omar Khash is the M.C. as well as the comic, an oily, cheerful, fat man in an oversized turban. He's onstage, holding a mike in one hand, a phallic-looking balloon sword in the other. He swings the balloon a few times, milking a previous laugh, and then begins my introduction. It's a big bullshitty buildup – American singing sensation! The continental Joan Baez! (What continent *is* that, exactly?) and star of Broadway musicals! I'm on to a wave of applause. I can see only the candles on each table, hundreds of tiny beacons.

There is a seduction between singer and audience. On some nights, both can be shy, uncertain. Nervousness rises into my throat, lending my voice a hoarse edge. I select one candlelit table and sing to the invisible people, inviting them with my voice. They like the Jacques Brel songs, even in my uncertain French, and my traditional American folk songs, in the lower, huskier key Monsieur Frochot had suggested. The applause is gratifying, if not the fervent standing ovation of my dreams.

"Ah but you are wonderful!" Meskat exclaims, when I'm back in my dressing room. He reflexively straightens a framed poster on the wall. "But perhaps if I may make a suggestion?" He pauses for my nod of resigned acceptance. "You could sing more songs that are a little bit familiar to our audience. A favorite of mine is "Michael Row Your Boat Ashore Hallelujah." You could sing that."

"I could sing that."

This pleases him. Valerie Marchand's musical introduction begins.

I slip out the side door and make my way around to the back of the club to watch her. The two men I'd seen smoking hash in the hallway earlier are Valerie's bass player and drummer. With the pianist, they kick up a swinging arrangement of "From This Moment On," joined by the jazzy horn section of a twelve-piece band. Valerie is the kind of entertainer who stalks the stage, extends the microphone cord to its limits and goes into the audience, touching and flirting. She segues into Piaf's "Je Ne Regrette Rien" as I quietly exit the club, feeling outdone.

In my room, I turn on the television. There are three channels. One is playing a Persian variety show; another has a Farsi news program; the third, a rerun of *I Love Lucy*, dubbed in Farsi. Lucy and Ethel are pretending to be Martian women. When the episode ends, I put on my coat and take the elevator down to the lobby, continuing to the back exit.

The wide patio behind the hotel is deserted. Music from the club throbs through the walls. Night has brought out a million stars and a glowing moon. The air is arid and arctic. The wind kicks up sand and leaves, stray cocktail napkins.

Max and the others are probably at some cozy café, arguing over the political landscape. I've never been especially political. I'm against the war in Vietnam – who isn't? – and I once took part in a demonstration at Columbia University, mainly because I was dating a radical student. The protest seemed like a bold thing to do, but I was bored before an hour had elapsed. Trudging in a circle carrying a placard, sitting on the cold stone steps in winter, and having to listen to everyone talk about the "pigs" and the "corrupt establishment" is tiresome in the extreme. I told my friend I had to find a bathroom, and just kept walking, across the campus to the nearest subway station.

Maybe I should have stuck it out, and learned something.

The terrace faces the northern part of the city and the mountains. What is Afghanistan like? Iraq? Where is Harry tonight? Oh, would I never stop thinking of him, holding conversations with him in my head?

Harry, look where I am, look at the way the moonlight glows on Mount Damavond!

It's almost as tall as the Himalayas.

I read the guidebook, Harry. He touches my hair. *Let's go upstairs and try out that Jacuzzi. I want to see you naked. I've missed you. I want to tie you up and make you wait, and hear you scream with pleasure.*

The hotel's outdoor swimming pool is closed for the winter and covered by a tarp. There is an indoor one I plan to try. *Where shall we go first, Harry? The bazaars? You'd go to the art museum.* I'm near the low steps that lead down to the gardens.

"Miss Bell!"

Omar Khash lumbers toward me. A black wool cloak covers much of his form, flying in the breeze like the wings of a large ungainly bird. "I like your show, Miss Bell."

"Call me Rebecca."

"Rebecca, pretty name, from the Bible, yes? You are a singer of some talent! I dig the guitar, it's a groove. I play a little, well, that's what everybody tells me to do – play a little! Or not at all!" He pauses for a breath, and rattles on, "Wish I could sing like Frank Sinatra! Or even Frank Sinatra, Jr.! When I was in Vegas, I hung out with the cats in Frank Jr.'s band, you know, Frank Jr.'s just as talented as his poppa, but there can't be two of them, believe me, I know, my poppa is Mali Khash, the Shi'ite Comedy King – just kidding, but you probably wouldn't know that they've got no sense of humor those Shi'ites! Not like the Jews! Are you a Jewess?"

"Well…no—"

He speaks right over me. "Ah, too bad, I like the Jewess American Princess. I fell in love with a girl back in Vegas, a showgirl, but it turned out she didn't like Iranians, or maybe it is just me she didn't like! Hahahaha! American women are very difficult to please! You are an especially beautiful American woman, and I would like very much to invite you to dinner in my room!"

"Well, actually—"

"I know. I'm too fat! That is why the women don't dig me! That's no problem, we will eat in the dining room with the fat rich tourists and I will blend in!" He sticks his hand into the folds of his cloak and pulls out a cigarette case and a matchbook. He lights two cigarettes and hands one to me.

"I don't smoke."

"And here I am pretending to be the man in the Bette Davis movie, and feeling like a fool!" He brushes the ember off the extra cigarette and slips it back into the case. His stubby fingers tweak the matchbook, flicking it back and forth; tic tic. "Please, if I may have the pleasure of your company, I will be your love slave! I will shower you with gifts and expect no favors in return. I will tell funny jokes and many that are not so funny! I will buy you a martini with an olive!"

"I prefer those tiny onions."

"Then you shall have a dozen! Say yes!"

"Yes, for heaven's sake," I said, not sure what I've said yes to.

Omar Khash grabs my hand, leads me down the steps to the garden. A bower arches over the walkway, the branches bare in winter.

"Pretty night, isn't it? Amazing to think about the many wars that have been fought in this land, all the history." His voice drops into a more serious tone. The comic persona is gone. "I'm an amateur archeologist, and this part of the world fascinates me. I always think of all the

71

thousands of years of buried bones out there in the desert." He lights a match, blows it out, drops it, lights another.

I step back but he moves closer to me.

"Zand Bahador," he whispers.

Crowds spill out on to the terrace, smoking, laughing.

"What?"

Omar Khash bows. "Goodnight, Rebecca, it was nice conversing with you."

And he is gone.

He must be the "contact" that Chris Fargate mentioned. Why was he so cryptic about it? Testing me out, I guess. I'll call Chris tomorrow at the gallery.

In the corridor to my room, the light flickers, spits, and goes out. I try to fit the room key into the lock several times before it catches, and I rush in and slam the door behind me and double lock the door.

Something isn't right. I turn on all the lights. My suitcase was on the closet floor when I left. Now it's in the hall next to the bathroom. I quickly rummage through my stuff. Nothing is missing.

The figurine! I'd put it in the guitar case, in the closet. It's still there. I pull apart the wrapping. The little face, with its blue-jeweled eyes, glitters, almost inquisitive. I examine the thing again for anything I might not have noticed; a hidden compartment or a marking. It is smooth and unblemished. There is no secret hidden inside. It's just an artifact. An ordinary dealer in London and an equally ordinary dealer in Paris have sent it to Iran, admittedly in an unconventional way and certainly skirting the law, in order to sell it. That's all there is to it. Probably a housekeeper was in the room, tidying up. The bed has been turned down. Odd that the suitcase would be out of place, but perhaps she got interrupted. There's even a gold-wrapped chocolate on the pillow. I've become too suspicious. Still, I make sure the door is double locked, and the patio door, with the brocade curtains closed tight.

16

In the morning, I try Chris at the gallery but there's no answer. Leaving the hotel, I breathe in the heady freedom of being in a strange city and having a day to explore it. I've decided to give the figurine to Khash the next time I see him or leave it at the front desk for him, with a note. Just making the decision is a relief.

Tehran is many cities in one. Mosque minarets glint in the sun, dwarfed by new high-rise office buildings. The streets are immaculate, the main boulevards as wide as the Champs Élysées. I walk south, in a pair of old, friendly red Keds, their color heightening my illusion of being Dorothy in Oz. The day is mild, the sun near the top of the sky, a light that seems filtered through some ancient scrim.

A few women in chadors flow past, flouting the new restrictions that outlawed religious garments. Many more wear dresses and fashionable coats indistinguishable from those in New York or Paris, although some wear the hijab, a kerchief folded over the hair and around the neck. Men sport caps, turbans, Arab headdresses, and long flowing robes. Others are in crisp-tailored business suits.

Street vendors tend their food stalls, offering aromatic varieties of sweets and fresh- baked breads and meats. The exotic spice mixture in the air makes me hungry. The vendors beckon, offering samples, and I taste meat of unknown origin, delicate pastry, and rosewater-fragrant breads, still warm from the oven.

Narrow, deep waterways carry water from the mountains, falling into streams that snake their way to the densely crowded areas of the city, where it is polluted by the streets and yet used for fishing and for drinking.

A sound in the distance rises and falls, expands into hundreds of voices calling out the same phrase over and over. Another voice, in counterpoint, roars through a bullhorn, the hollow shout dopplering as if the source were moving.

I approach what the tour booklet informs me is the center of the city. The splendorous Golestan palace rises like a dream from my childhood, when I had worn out the pages of fairy tales. A sign says that no visitors are allowed in the palace that day; the royal family is in residence. I visualize them reclining on velvet sofas, being fed fruit by servants, knowing that in reality they are a modern, sophisticated family like the Rainiers of Monaco.

The voices draw closer, the chanting louder. A jet swoops overhead and then another, leaving vapor trails in its wake. The planes loop and return, lower now, the engine drone nearly drowning the shouts. My father's voice in my head advises me to go the other way, and my mother adds that I'm asking for trouble, which is nothing new; trouble and curiosity pull with a magnet's force. When I was a kid, I *had* to see each horrible detail of a terrible car accident that had happened outside our house. After the ambulances had gone, and the neighbors were back in their homes, soothing themselves with coffee and booze, I sneaked outside, dusk falling, to stare at the blood on the pavement.

It's too late to turn around. Like a wave, the multitude surges around the corner, placards bouncing in the air. A flatbed truck moves slowly by and I see the man with the bullhorn, exhorting the crowd. They're mostly young, an excitable horde, not unlike the student protest marchers back home, but instead of pictures of Agent Orange victims, peace symbols, the skewed images of Nixon, of Kissinger, these demonstrators wield effigies of the shah and even more gruesome photos of tortured bodies, maimed limbs, smashed faces – their features distorted, un-human. I recognize one word, yelled over and over; Sa-vak, Sa-vak – the secret police. One sign shows an American flag with blood on it. Our government is not well-loved here, and our oil companies even less so.

Soldiers on horseback appear as if conjured from some magician's wand, and form a line barricading, surrounding the palace. From across the square, a new group emerges; men in robes and head wrappings, brandishing sticks, small swords, whatever they can carry and use as a weapon. The women follow, indistinguishable and hidden behind veils, creating a ululation that pierces the ears. The crowd pushes forward, defying the soldiers. The fortified line of horses parts at the approach of a hellish tank, and another behind it.

The two mobs merge and swell and there is no exit, just bodies, screaming, chanting, and the unremitting war cries of the veiled women.

I stumble backwards, kept upright by close-packed people, and feel something tear at my clothes. Hands grab at me, a cloaked mouth shrieking some ancient curse. There's a break in the crowd, and I shove a path toward it, managing to elude the tormentors that had targeted me; the stranger, the corrupt Western woman. My sneakered feet slap the pavement and jump over a fallen body. As I pass the last of the religious demonstrators, a soldier gallops toward a robed woman at the edge of the crowd and smashes his club down on her head. The woman collapses, soundlessly. The soldier reins his horse and looks at me. "Go home, Miss," he says in accented English.

I run until the screams, the popping bullets disappear. The air is thick with smoke and dust, the narrow streets twisting into side alleys. I bump into a donkey cart and apologize to the driver, an old man wrapped in rags, his skin dark and creased as old leather. The cart is laden with intricately designed Persian rugs.

"You buy?" He stops the cart. The donkey hangs its head in resignation. "Good price."

"No money." My purse is hidden, strapped around my shoulder and under my coat, a theft precaution learned the hard way in New York City. The carpet seller tries a few more times, then shrugs and moves on. The cart jangles down the street, swallowed by throngs of people, cars, wagons.

Shops and stalls line the streets of the bazaar, continuing for miles. Merchandise of amazing value – or none at all. Jewels, coffees, teas, spices, carpets, silks, wool, goats, sheep, alive and bleating or dead and hanging. Mosaic tiles catch the sun and flash it back. Shoppers bump into one another in their eagerness to sample the wares. A man urinates into the gutter, oblivious to the people passing by.

There are other Western tourists, and this is a relief. I'm unused to the scrutiny of being different. The delayed shock of the demonstration and riot is beginning to set in. I lean against a stone wall, rough and uneven on my back, and put my hands over my face. For the first time, I really want to go home. But where is home?

An apparition approaches, a tall woman swathed in a thick, gray wool cloak, her long, pale hair escaping from a shawl that drapes from the top of her head to well below her knees. Her eyes shine bright blue, and her graceful fingers pick at the offerings at a vegetable stand. The woman whispers something to the vendor and he laughs in an insinuating way. I follow her, curious. We get to an alley that leads away from the center of the bazaar. Sewage drifts down the gutters, giving off a stench that makes me wish I had a scarf covering my nose and mouth. The woman sees me and turns.

Her face is pretty but fatigued, with shadows like bruises beneath her eyes. She looks to be around my age, maybe a few years older. With a silver-ringed hand, she reaches into her bag, pulls out a small bag of dates, and offers me one.

It's intensely sweet. I begin to laugh, out of control. "Sorry, I'm a little shook up. There was a riot, a mob…I thought I was going to be crushed."

"Yeah I heard it. Bummer."

Mounted police clatter past the alley. She grimaces. "Fascists. Religious fanatics. Can't tell which is worse. This whole fucking country is getting so uncool. Have you been here long?"

"A week. I'm singing at the Diamond International."

Her eyebrows raise. "What's your sign?"

"What? Oh, Gemini."

"Ah." She nods meaningfully. "I'm Scorpio. But my rising sign is Gemini."

I also nod meaningfully. "Where are you from? I mean, you're American, right?"

"I don't really think of being from anywhere, you know? What does it mean to say you're *from* Iowa or Texas or Montreal…..or the moon? That just divides people and causes wars. We're all from the same universal consciousness, right? But, to answer your question, oh god no, not American. Canadian. Shitty time to be American, with the war and all, and your horrible president. Oh, I'm sorry, maybe you like him! I'm such an idiot!"

"No, I don't like him either. Or the war."

She reaches again into her copious bag, pulls out a small hash pipe and lights it. At my anxious glance around, she adds, "Don't worry, nobody gives a shit."

I take a long hit, hold it down and cough. "Holy shit."

"No shit. I got it in Afghanistan. Amazing place," she says. "I just got back. There's this commune of incredibly cool people into understanding on a deeper level."

Every cultist imagines he or she is uncovering some universal truth. But maybe I'm judging her too harshly.

"Hey, I'm Trish."

"Rebecca." We shake hands.

"I gotta be going." She scrawls an address on a scrap of paper from her bag and hands it to me. "Here's our address. There's no phone, just come by any time. I share the house with a couple of guys. No, not like that!" She laughs and heads back toward the main street, turns to wave at me, and is swallowed by the crowd.

The hash is stronger than any I've ever had in my life. As I make my way back to the bazaar, the colors become brighter and the noises sharper and more defined. A peddler crouches on the ground next to his wagon, puffing on a hookah, the liquid burbling in the base, white smoke curling up and evaporating into a pale blue sky. Has it been minutes since I left Trish? An hour? Did I even meet a woman named Trish? How stupid to take drugs from a stranger. There's something about being in a foreign country that induces a blind and foolish trust. When it should be just the opposite.

I need to get back to the hotel, but my sense of direction is more distorted than usual. A relentless hammering comes from inside my head but it's a bazaari pounding copper into the shape of a plate. The stalls are so close together they fill every space. The pounding subsides to a throb like a distant heartbeat and disappears into the muted thickness of carpets, dozens piled one upon the other, on tables, on the ground, and hung in long rows like brilliantly colored sound buffering. The bazaar winds on and on without an exit; a maze that eventually reveals a sliver of light.

I walk towards the domes of the palace in the distance. The city is organized and even familiar, the streets around the palace quiet, pristine. Soldiers and police guards patrol, but there is little evidence that anything out of the ordinary has occurred. The wind scatters a cluster of discarded, torn leaflets. A custodian wields a thick water hose and the gutters stream pink, carrying the refuse and blood down and away from the city.

17

The effects of the hash are wearing off by the time I see the hotel in the distance.

There are three letters waiting for me at the hotel desk. One is from Max, the other from Alistair, and the third appears to be an invitation. I open that one first.

> *Mademoiselle Rebecca Bell:*
> *You are most cordially invited to a dinner party my husband and I are hosting at our home next Sunday evening at 8:00 PM. We enjoyed your performance last week and would like to welcome you as our guest.*
> *M. et Mme. Nareem Mirsheidaie*
> *RSVP*

A small card and envelope are enclosed for the reply. Both the card and letter have a rich, silky feel, the sender's address embossed in silver. I've never heard of these people, but it sounds fancy and fun.

Max's letter is written on wafer-thin blue airmail paper.

> *Dear Rebecca,*
>
> *Paris is lonely without you, there is no other way to say it. The lyrebirds still aren't singing. Please write and tell me about your adventures in Persia. It must be a wonderful new world for a home-schooled religious fanatic-turned-atheist (I kid, of course). Jimmy sends his regards. Ellen, too (yes, really).*
>
> *Fondly,*
>
> *Max*

The third is on Alistair's gallery stationary. There's a newspaper clipping, and a folded note with a short message:

> I thought you should see this if you haven't already received the sad news. A.

Art Collector Found Dead
Christopher Fargate, 43, a Paris art dealer, was found dead in his gallery, apparently of a heart attack. Fargate opened his gallery in 1967 and specialized in Persian antiquities.

When I get to the club that evening, I discover that there is a new comic/MC.

Meskat offers me a cursory nod and a tight smile. "You are late, Miss Bell. I wish you would be early and not to worry me."

"Sorry. What happened to Omar Khash?"

He purses his lips. "A family emergency. We regret to lose him but happy to get Hamoud, who is luckily between bookings."

Omar Khash, who said "Zand" to me. Or had I misheard him? We were staring out at a distant desert, and he could have said "sand." No, he said "Zand Bahador." Now Khash has departed, if not this world, then at least Tehran. And I still have the damned thing.

Hamoud is trying too hard to make the audience laugh. No mystery why he's available on short notice. On the way to my dressing room, I pass Valerie Marchand, gaudily resplendent in a green, feather-trimmed satin robe.

Hamoud winds up his show and goes into my introduction, "Rebecca Ball," he announces, getting my name wrong.

I sing on automatic pilot, while thinking of Chris Fargate; a man for whom I had few feelings while he was alive but feel strangely compassionate towards now that he is dead.

After the first show, I find Meskat. "Do you know of a Nareem Mirsheidaie?" I stumble over the pronunciation.

His eyebrows rise and he corrects me. "'Meer-shed-eye.' A very rich man. He and his wife come here frequently and always tip many rials!"

"What does he do?"

"A large importing and exporting business, if I am correct. He also buys and sells art, the very expensive kind that I cannot afford. Why do you ask?"

"He and his wife invited me to a party."

"Of course! They were here for your show recently. Lucky you!" His smile is forced, then turns suggestive. "Perhaps they are intrigued by your performance in a famous sex musical."

He's probably right. That show is both a curse and an entrée. I'm defined by it forever, but I'm also grateful that it renders me more interesting and rather bawdy.

My journey to taking off my clothes onstage began inauspiciously in early 1969, after a giant snowstorm that had left the streets of New York piled high with graying icy mountains.

There were two show business trade papers. The respectable one, *Backstage*, would list shows, chorus calls and films that were casting each week. The other, *Show Business*, included boxed ads for "Models/Escorts

Wanted - Hi Pay," and auditions for obscure, non-union dinner-theater tours where you'd have to wait tables before jumping onstage to perform in the show.

Show Business's casting page featured this ad:

The Sound of One Hand Clapping by A. Starling. Seeking young, attractive, female folksinger/guitar player to sing before the show, perform in ensemble. Some pay.

On the evening of the audition, I took the city's most dilapidated subway – the L line – from my Lower East Side roach trap to 14th and Sixth. During the day, this was a teeming sidewalk flea market of cheap merchandise, crummy storefronts, and passed-out drunks. At night it was pretty much deserted, except for the drunks. Lugging my guitar, I climbed up the subway steps, out onto the empty, dark street in my high black boots, trying not to slip on the ice or sink into the snowdrifts. I didn't wear a hat, for the sake of vanity, and it was four degrees outside, with a notable wind chill.

The Actors Arts Theatre was a fourth-floor walkup, each creaking step apparently installed by different carpenters with varied spatial skills. On the top floor, there was a narrow room crowded with about fifteen women clutching guitars. Some were not what I would categorize as young, or attractive. A theater poster taped to the wall had an illustration of a shadowy couple, apparently nude, making love: *The Sound of One Hand Clapping*, a new drama by A. Starling. Starring A. Starling and Stephen Grant. Produced and directed by A. Starling and Stephen Grant. Held Over!

An hour and a half later, my turn came. The theater was a wide, shallow space, all black walls and black ceilings and floor, with black velvet curtains partitioning the wings and a backstage area, with about fifty shabby seats that must have once graced a venerable movie palace.

Two people sat behind a table piled high with pictures and resumes.

An elderly woman, with frizzy magenta hair, thick pancake makeup, abundant ruby lipstick, and a clatter of bracelets on crepey, age-spotted arms. Next to her was a wraithlike man in his thirties or forties, his thinning brown hair carefully combed over, and a long woolen scarf wound around his neck, in the chokingly hot room. A steam radiator on the far wall hissed and spit and clanked like Marley's ghost.

"Hellooo," he said in the mellifluous tones of a Person of the Theatre. "I'm Stephen Grant. And this is Anastasia Starling." He tipped his head back, regarding me, squinting, lips pursed, left eyebrow lifted. "So, darling! What are you going to sing for us?"

"What sort of songs are you looking for?"

"Something *sen*-sual," the woman replied. "Our play is a study in ero*t*icism, an exploration of the transcendence of love in a cold, modern world."

I decided on "Summertime." As soon as my last note trailed away, Stephen Grant stood and applauded. "My *dear*! What a lovely voice you have."

Anastasia went right to the point. "There is some tasteful nudity in our play and a spec*tac*ular, psyche*del*ic orgy scene. Of course, you would not be required to participate, unless you so choose. And it all takes place under strobe lighting. My play is a *big* hit, you know. We've been running for six months, and there is a waiting list for tickets. You would be replacing our wonderful Sonya, who has been cast in *Hair*!"

I had already auditioned for *Hair*, but was not offered a part, despite my having very long hair.

Stephen Grant winked. "We'll be in touch."

The phone was ringing as I walked through my apartment door. Stephen Grant. "We would *so* love for you to join our little company."

I was flattered out of proportion to the actual job, rather desperate for approval after a long fallow period. "Yes," I said, stomping on a roach skittering across the linoleum.

"Some pay" amounted to ten dollars a week. About two dollars a performance.

The Sound of One Hand Clapping starred Anastasia and Stephen as lovers who undressed several times over the course of the play and simulated lovemaking. The cast was a ragtag bunch of way-off-off Broadway actors, who liked to get high backstage and laugh at the pairing of the two leads, both of whom were gay. The sole reason the play had an unprecedented six-month run was because of the big sex scene, which was, thankfully, performed in dim light, and was followed by a Bacchanalian strobe-lit "orgy," in which the entire cast rushed onstage, either nude or wearing diaphanous gowns, and went at each other in a frenzy of simulated sex.

The first time I watched this, my mind turned into a war zone of conflicting emotions. What would my family have thought?

"Then the eyes of both of them were opened, and they knew that they were naked; and they sewed fig leaves together and made themselves loin coverings." Genesis.

I imagined myself making loin coverings for the entire cast. Back in the dressing room, I waited in shame for the scene to end. When everyone came rushing in, naked and laughing, I tried to make myself invisible. But, no, they could see me.

"Rebecca, you *have* to do it!" This from one of the more flamboyant gay men. "You'll be liberated!"

"Um, maybe next weekend." Or maybe not. I'd probably have my period.

But they were having so much fun.

After watching from the wings for several more performances, I could not resist any longer. I put on one of the transparent cloaks, slipped off everything underneath but my underwear, took a deep breath and joined them center stage. One of the actors put his arms around me and writhed close. I leaned back, smiling up at the stage lights. The next performance, I left off the underwear.

It was this wonderfully dreadful show that inspired me to audition for *Au Naturel!* a few months later.

18

On the night of the Mirsheidaie dinner party, the taxi races me past the palace, continues several more blocks, and turns onto a street thick with old trees, to a long driveway. The estate encompasses an expanse of perfect lawn, a grove of date palms and walnut trees, and elaborate topiary animals. Ringed around the garden are half a dozen alabaster Roman statues, with the chipped noses and amputated limbs of authentic relics.

A butler takes my coat. I'm wearing a silver lamé cocktail dress I bought in Paris, the material embracing my body like a luminous membrane. Nareem Mirsheidaie, a stocky man in his fifties with a wide, gray-flecked mustache and a firm handshake, takes me in with just the barest glimpse, but I feel as if I've had been stripped and fucked in that split second. His American wife, Eleanor, is a thin, blonde beauty with pointy features and tanned legs, muscled from semi-pro tennis. (I later find a glass cabinet with Eleanor's tennis trophies.)

In the living room, a jazz trio plays subdued pop standards on piano, upright bass, and guitar.

The dozen or so guests include the American ambassador, John Berringer, and his wife, Lisa; a young Pakistani or Indian, Dr. Jalil

Mookerji; a thickset, red-haired military type named Kyle Mac-something; and a statuesque woman in a tuxedo. Her burgundy hair is pulled back in a severe chignon that makes her sharp-cut features more prominent. Black eyes tilt up slightly at the corners, hinting at some Asian or Tartar ancestry.

Evelyn Mirsheidaie introduces us. "Rebecca, this is Clementine Solis."

"I've heard so much about you," Clementine says, with a trace of an accent. "I've been meaning to catch your show, but I've been traveling so much. I used to play Irish harp, but just don't have time anymore."

"She's actually quite good," Evelyn says. "Played at Covent Garden."

Clementine waves her hands. "Oh, a university orchestra concert when I was quite young!"

Evelyn says, "Clementine is at the Iranian Consulate in Paris." Turning to her, "I don't know just what it is you do, Clem." In a stage whisper to me, "But I think she's a spy!"

"Just a low-level diplomat, I'm afraid. Evelyn has a wild imagination."

"And of course," Evelyn says, "Rebecca will sing for us."

Well at least now I know why I was invited. I've discovered that the richest people try to get everything for free.

The elaborate dining room table is set for fourteen, the Mirsheidaies at the head and foot. There are name cards at the place settings for each of the guests. As we all find our places, I notice that there is one empty chair at the other end of the table.

Before taking her seat, Evelyn Mirsheidaie whispers something to her husband, glancing at the empty chair. He shrugs and kisses her on the cheek. Evelyn frowns and whisks the name card off the table, handing it to one of the servers.

A parade of delicacies and wines begins.

Evelyn, now two chairs away from me, asks if I'm familiar with Persian dishes. When I shake my head, she tells me about each one. There is a tiny beet and feta cheese tart; a *borani*, which mixes yogurt and vegetables; sliced roasted eggplant with pomegranate and mint dressing; *dolmeh bargeh mo* (stuffed grape leaves); and generous portions of *lavash* bread.

The tablecloth is a smooth linen in alternating shades of pale blue and white. I'm not sure which fork to pick up first and look at the others for a cue.

Two servers roll in carts, each bearing the main course on covered silver platters. In unison, they lift the covers, revealing roast lamb dusted with herbs and pomegranate, on a bed of saffron rice. The guests raise their glasses.

I'm not fond of meat. My face must show it because when I meet the eyes of the Pakistani-or-Indian, Dr. Mookerji, seated directly across the table, he nods toward the lamb, puffs out his cheeks in mock queasiness, and shudders. "You are also vegetarian?" he asks, in a flat, almost unaccented English.

"Well, I prefer not to eat mammals. But it's difficult when you're traveling and want to try things."

"I won't tell the mammals."

"You're young to be a doctor, Doctor Mookerji. I mean that in a good way."

"Call me Jalil, please. And I'm not a medical doctor, but a lowly PhD. I recently finished my physics doctorate, in the Netherlands. You know the American expression, 'it doesn't take a rocket scientist'? Well, I am the rocket scientist it doesn't take." He breaks his dinner roll in two, removes the soft inner dough, squeezes it into a ball, and puts it aside.

I ask him where he's from and realize that's probably a pushy American question. "Sorry, didn't mean to be nosy."

"Not at all! I was born in India, but my family went to Pakistan when I was very young, and then we moved to Iran so that my father could teach in the university. I consider this my home."

The waiters carve the meat and move silently around the table, serving it from platters.

"So, my dear," Kyle, the Scot, says, "What brings you to this part of the worrrld?" The backs of his freckled hands are furred with golden hairs.

Clementine leans over. "Kyle, you *are* out of the loop. Rebecca is our chanteuse in residence at the International."

Jalil Mookerji brightens. "A singer! I'm honored to meet you! Any artist is a refreshing change from academics and think-tank bureaucrats."

Laughter erupts at the other end of the table. "…and the goat ran away!" Nareem exclaims, face flushed. The ambassador and his wife join in the laughter.

"When is your next show?" Kyle asks.

"I have one later tonight."

The meat-bearing servant comes to me. To be polite, I let him place a slice of dead mammal on my plate.

"Are you enjoying Iran, Miss Bell?" Jalil Mookerji asks. "Have you gotten to see much of it?"

"I did wander around the city. Right into the middle of a riot. Well, a demonstration that turned into a riot."

"I'm sure it wasn't a riot," one of the Iranian guests says, with a frown. "We don't have those."

I decide not to contradict him.

"That must have been very frightening," Kyle says. "You need to be more careful."

I feign an offhand tone. "Oh, it's just like home – the anti-war demonstrations. Although I'm not quite sure what people here are for or against."

Kyle is happy to enlighten me. "It's not so different from your hairy radicals and student dissidents in the States, who think they can take down a government. The only difference is that in Iran they might actually pull it off one day."

"That could never happen here," Evelyn insists.

Jalil laughs, with an angry edge.

I look at him. "But I thought the Shah had made things more modern. Better."

He leans toward me and speaks quietly. "To most Americans, 'modern' is synonymous with 'better.' But not to the religious factions in this part of the world. The Shiite clergy do not care for the shah's American-style reforms. They think everyone is going to end up an atheist, and their women and girls will disobey their fathers and go off and have sex and listen to rock and roll. That Iran will be run by gangsters and Hollywood." He picks up the ball of bread dough, and when he puts it down again, I can see the imprints of his fingers.

"Think about the workers," he continues. "The Shah's 'reform' of agriculture means that millions lost their jobs in the countryside and had to come to the city to find jobs that pay even less. Or no jobs at all. They crowd into slums a few blocks from where the millionaires live. A reminder every day of what they don't have." He gestures to the mansion around them. "The elite get richer and the poor get poorer, which, I suppose, is the story of history. The Shah's secret police, the SAVAK, torture and kill those who speak up, who try to have the kind of 'human rights' America is always shouting about. But who supports SAVAK? America –"

Kyle breaks in. "The dispassionate scientist speaks. When he should probably shut up."

The pleasant expression disappears from Jalil Mookerji's eyes. His calm voice masks rage. "Americans and the United Kingdom and the West have bought the governments of this country and many others. Any country with oil. You give us weapons and get angry when we want to use them. Your country gives the world McDonald's and Barbie dolls and fake television laugh tracks. America is like Rome, and we all know what happened to Rome. And Iran is Russia in 1914."

"Whoa," I say. "It's not my fault. My parents wouldn't even let me have a Barbie doll." Actually, I was a little too old when Barbie came along. But they would have considered her to be sinful. *Little children, keep yourselves from idols. 1 John 5:21*

Jalil's demeanor softens. "If only all Americans were as delightful as you are, Miss Bell." He reached across and touches my hand, gently. "I apologize. I don't dislike Americans because I don't confuse the American people with the American leaders like Mr. Nixon and Mr. Kissinger. But there are many in the world that do not make that distinction."

"Your parents wouldn't let you have a Barbie doll?" Clementine has an expression of mock horror.

"We were very religious. I wasn't allowed to dance or listen to secular music or go to the movies or to regular schools." I realize the room has gone silent and everyone is looking at me.

Clementine regards me with curiosity. "You are Christian?"

I nod, but I'm not sure anymore.

"A fundamentalist Christian?" she adds.

I had never thought of it that way. "Well, we believe – believed – in the Bible as the word of God."

"And your god is the only god? Or the only proper god?" Jalil says, with a teasing smile.

I flush. "I guess so." Of course ours is the only god! Jesus is the One True God. Isn't He? My mind goes to this belief like a homing pigeon. No, I don't believe that anymore. But it feels so safe to believe without question.

Jalil laughs. "And here all along I am thinking Mohammed is the true prophet."

A man at the end of the table pipes up, with a smile, "No, no, Moses is the one prophet. Our Bible came first, after all."

"Yes," says Clementine, "but you are a sabra Israeli, and that is an entirely different kind of Jew."

The man stands up, his chair pushing back with a scrape. "Any Jew who comes to Israel is the true Jew. I—"

Mirsheidaie jumps in, "And do we have a Hindu to round out this assemblage? No? I am remiss in our guest list."

I blurt out, "All I wanted was a Barbie doll." There is laughter.

"And yet," the American attaché's wife, says, "these days that is not very feminist."

"Oh, for heaven's sake," Evelyn Mirsheidaie says, "must we solve all the problems of the world tonight?" She signals one of the servants. "I suggest we have dessert."

Kyle raises his glass. "To women's liberation." His tone is sardonic.

Jalil is clearly unimpressed but lifts his glass with a cynical shrug.

Nareem Mirsheidaie offers one final toast. "To all our wonderful and diverse international guests. May there be peace in the world." And in Farsi, "*Be salamati!*"

After dinner, the Mirsheidaies ask me to sing a couple of songs. The jazz trio doesn't know much of my repertoire, but they know a lot of American standards, and we eventually agree on songs, keys, and tempos. If this were a movie, an orchestra would launch into a complicated arrangement that everyone knows perfectly.

We stumble through a sultry, romantic "When I Fall in Love" and a bouncy version of "They All Laughed." The guests applaud and ask for another. By this time, we've found a balance, and riff a jazzy "Summertime."

The party moves into a ballroom with a gleaming wooden floor. The jazz ensemble has added a few more musicians – a drummer and horn section – and they kick up a dance beat. More guests join the party after dinner. Kyle spins me around the dance floor in classic ballroom style.

"For a girl forbidden to dance," he says, "you've picked up a few moves."

"When I escaped to New York City, I went to classes. Jazz, ballet, ballroom. I couldn't get enough of it."

"The classes paid off." Kyle turns me and executes a graceful dip. "How long are you staying in Tehran?"

"I'm booked for one more month, but my agent says they want me to sign on for longer."

"You should go back to Europe, make a record. An old pal of mine works at EMI in Paris. I could set you up with a meeting."

"Really? Maybe you should be my agent."

"Does that mean I get ten percent of you?"

I deflect this with a laugh. "How can I contact your EMI friend? Do you have a card?"

He pats his pockets. "No, sorry, all out."

The usual bullshit. "What brings *you* to Iran?"

"This and that." Kyle spins me out, and back again. He's quite the dancer.

The song ends. Eleanor Mirsheidaie asks me to dance to a slow tune. She pulls me uncomfortably close. "I hope you'll visit us again very soon."

To my relief, the band takes a break. It's nearly time for me to leave, if I'm going to make my show. Evelyn tells one of the servants to have the chauffeur drive me to the hotel.

The night air has an icy, cruel edge. As the limo heads down the long driveway, another limo is approaching, in a hurry. The late guest?

The topiary animals lining the road rear and wave.

19

The club is packed, mostly with a large American tour group that's already had too much to drink. They're an exhausting audience. I keep the set upbeat, with familiar pop songs they can sing along to. It's not as bad as Le Scorpion, but it's the kind of show that makes me question my career choice. Afterward, I stop in the lounge for a drink, and consider calling Max, but I'm not sure what time it is in Paris.

People keep coming up to me, saying nice things about the show. Men want to buy me drinks and invite me to join them at the bar, in the dining room, in their rooms. No, and no, and no. I smile and laugh but loneliness is a heavy stone in my heart. Did I make a fool of myself at the Mirsheidaie party? Just a silly American female who knows nothing of international affairs? I am so out of my league with these people. Harry once called me an autodidact. Of course, I didn't know the word then and suspected it was an insult. I looked it up later; a self-taught person.

The window is wide open in my hotel room, a cold breeze billowing the curtains. I'm sure I left it closed. The light from outside casts a stream of illumination, just enough to define a silhouette.

Harry Lamb leans against the wall by the window, a cigarette in one hand, a drink in the other.

I freeze in the doorway.

"Hello, Rebecca."

This must be a hallucination. Or someone's idea of a joke, sending a Harry imposter.

"You can come in, you know," he says. "It's your room."

My legs seem to have gone numb because I can't move. My shaking hand reaches for the light switch.

Yes, it really is him, not a ghost. "Harry?"

He crushes the cigarette in an ashtray and comes toward me.

I back up. "What in God's name are you doing here?"

"You didn't think I could ever forget you?" His dark-gold hair is longer, his body leaner, the high cheekbones more defined. He needs a shave and there are new lines around his eyes.

"Well, yes, that's exactly what I thought. Why would I think any different?"

"I know." He hangs his head, half-mocking. "I'm an arsehole of major proportions."

"I think we can agree on that."

He sits on the sofa, stretching his arms out along the back. "For Christ sake, Rebecca, come here."

I stay in the doorway. "How did you get in my room?"

"Friendly maid."

A tan leather weekender bag is on the floor next to him.

He stands and comes towards me, extending a hand like he's approaching a feral animal. I take a step in, and close the door behind me, but put some distance between us. At the wet-bar I pour a drink from the first bottle my hand reaches. It's gin, which I loathe, but I would drink ammonia at this moment. He moves toward me again. The glass trembles in my hand. I put my other hand around it. A collision of emotions silences me again. Fury. Disbelief. Longing. More fury rescues me from the edge of weeping.

"Where have you been? Let's start there."

"Where haven't I been?"

I want to slap him. "It's what, three months? Four? I've lost track. Did you never in all that time come across a telephone or a postcard?"

"I can't tell you how many times I picked up the phone. But, well, things kept coming up. Not anything I'd want you involved in." He shakes his head. "And yet you got yourself mixed up with Fargate and Nelson and that crew."

"Mixed up? They're *your* friends, aren't they?" A chill goes through me. The Zand, wrapped, still in my suitcase.

"Friends? In the way that pythons are friends. It might feel cozy to have one wrapped around you – for about five seconds." He edges closer again. "Can't we hash all this out later? Rebecca, if you don't kiss me I think I will perish at your feet." He takes a flower from the vase and hands it to me.

"Fuck you."

He steps back. "No, you're right. I have no right. I'm such a fool to think you'd be glad to see me. Of course not, you've moved on. I'm so sorry."

Have I 'moved on'? If I could just think for a moment, but my head is scrambled with competing emotions. I take a long hard look at him. He's both a stranger and someone I know like the inside of my own mouth. All this time I've wondered, searched, raged, suffered. And here he is in the flesh.

He takes another tentative step toward me. When I don't move away this time, he touches my shoulder, gently.

The reality of him is waking from the dream and this time finding him here. "I don't know…"

"I know," he murmurs. He pulls me to him and kisses me until I'm certain I've dropped a few dozen IQ points. The reality of him, which I've thought of so many times, is a powerful aphrodisiac. It hasn't worn off. He caresses the back of my neck with his fingertips. "I'm so sorry. Forgive me."

Bowl of Night

I come to my senses and push him away. "Are you married?"

"What?"

"A wife. Do you have a family stashed someplace? If you do, just tell me. You wouldn't be my first married man, but I'd like to know."

He sighs. "No, I'm not married. I was… once, a long time ago. I told you the first night we met, along with how I hate all that commitment, where are you going, when'll you be home shite. You always seemed such a free spirit who isn't into all that."

A free spirit. Free love. A great idea, yet it never works out that way. There's always a cost. "You could have sent a fucking postcard."

He puts his hands up, in defense. "All right, I'm a shit-heel, I know that, I'm sorry, *mea culpa*, and let's see, I've screwed other women but I haven't made love, I was never *in* love, before you, and I didn't want to be, with you or with anyone, but I couldn't get you out of my head. I know that's a pretty tired line but it's true. *I fucking love you.* Will that do? Is that what you want to hear? Now will you come to bed with me?"

I'm vaguely aware of sirens down in the street. Arabic music drifts up. Reminders that there is a world outside this room. I'm supposed to swoon into his arms? Well, *fuck him*.

"Yes."

20

The room is pitch dark. For a moment, before I see him, I'm sure I've had a startling and wonderful dream. But, no, he is there, so still that I put my hand on his chest to be certain that his heart is beating.

The bed looks as if it hosted a wrestling match. In some ways it has. I was torn with desire and fury and took it out on him. Now, I'm exhausted and exhilarated all at once. Terrified he'll vanish again.

Harry opens his eyes, sees me, and smiles. "Hello. I thought I dreamed you." He gets up and pads into the bathroom, doesn't bother to shut the door. Ah, men. When he comes back he's wearing my complimentary robe. "Christ, I'm starving. You think there's room service at this hour?"

It's four-thirty in the morning.

"Twenty-four hours. The menu's on the desk." I get up quickly and grab the phone. "Wait, I'll do it. I have a reputation to protect here." He looks at me and we both burst out laughing.

Twenty minutes later, the food arrives. Steak. Potatoes. Coffee. Chocolate cake. We devour it all like we've never eaten before.

I sit on the bed, cross-legged, facing him. "Where the fuck did you go?"

He's still for a moment. "I left New York because I was having some business difficulties overseas and needed to straighten it all out. One thing led to another. It all got a lot more complicated than we expected." He shrugs. More silence. He rubs his eyes, gets up. "I need more coffee. Or a drink."

"No!" I pull him back to the bed.

"You scare me, Rebecca." He looks away. "Really you do. More than the crap I got myself into. I can't be worrying about you, and feeling like…like there's something…someone…who needs me. That's not the way I've lived my life."

"Then why are you here?" The sun is starting to come up, a raw edge of red on the horizon.

"Because I missed you." He looks at me now. "I know how trite that sounds. But I was almost on that Belgian plane out of Vienna that got hijacked. Took another one at the last minute. Such are the whims of the Great Whatever. I thought – I can't die without seeing Rebecca again."

"I thought you said you were in the Middle East."

"Right, I was, but I took a few side trips." He shakes his head, impatient. "Sweetheart, there's so much going on. I knew one of the athletes that died in the Black September attack on the Olympics. His father runs a small museum in Tel Aviv." He shakes his head. "Do we have to talk about all this? Look, I made some money, quite a lot, actually, and you and I can start over, if you'll have me."

He moves his hand to my breast. I feel my mind reeling back into a small space, and sensation taking its place. We're making love again, this time with less urgency and more tenderness. Slowly, meticulously, Harry worships my body, down between my legs and bringing me up to the brink and then backing off, repeating, until I am trembling all over, exploding into a world of ecstasy. He rolls over on his back. Whispers, "You taste like every wonderful thing on this earth."

We slept then.

The morning sun streaming in is a blinding reminder of reality. The memory of the night before, like so many other nights and memories, is as transient as a golden leaf blowing by on a winter day.

"Good morning, my pre-Raphaelite beauty." He is on his side, leaning on one elbow, looking at me.

"Oh god, I must look like post-Raphaelite shit."

He laughs and gets up, nude, picks up the phone for room service. Then hands it to me. "I forgot. Your reputation."

After breakfast, we shower and dress. There is an unease in the room. Neither of us knows what comes next.

Rummaging in the closet, I take out the wrapped figurine. "Harry, I have this…thing. I got it from Alis—"

He cuts me off. "I know."

The room is eerily still.

"You *know*?" I'm finding it hard to breathe. "*That's* why you're here?"

"Of course not."

There's a soft knock at the door. A woman's voice says, 'May I make up your room?"

"No, not right now!"

The cart rolls away down the hall. I unwrap the Zand and hand it to Harry. "Here, it's yours. I hope you got what you came for."

"That's not why I came here. I just knew Alistair gave it to you. No big deal." He takes it from me, turns it around and over and upright again. "Pretty," he murmurs.

"What is the great appeal, that everyone wants it? Is it worth a fortune? Does it have the Dead Sea Scrolls on microfilm inside? A secret code?"

"Rebecca, it's the equivalent of Mesopotamian motel art." That rakish smile.

I almost laugh.

Harry places it on the mirrored bar, facing us. Its little blue eyes sparkle. He regards it. "If this were a movie, it would be the MacGuffin."

I have no idea what he's talking about.

"A MacGuffin," he says, "is a…a plot device in a movie, a kind of decoy, important in the beginning but usually gets…I don't know – abandoned? – halfway through." He laughs. "I dated a movie producer in London who worked with Hitchcock. It's his term. I think." He looks proud of himself for coming up with this bit of trivia.

I go into the bathroom, slam the door, and lock it.

Harry follows, yelling from the other side. "I'm sorry! I was just joking around!"

"This is real life, not a fucking movie. Please, please take the damn… MacGuffin! I can't seem to get rid of it! I was supposed to turn it over to this comic but he just vanished. Oh, and someone was in my room one night when I was at the club." A war between rage and despair hammers inside my head. "And you know what you can do with it!"

"Rebecca—"

"Get the fuck out! And this time, don't come back." Now the tears are coming. I turn on the faucet as a sound barrier.

"Please, Rebecca, come out." When I don't reply, he continues. "There are some really nasty people out there. They…I'm…it's a bit of a mess." There's real emotion in his voice.

I turn off the water. "Like Chris Fargate?"

"He should have chucked it in the Seine."

"He died. A heart attack."

"That's the story."

"But you don't believe it?"

"Let's say I'm suspicious about the timing."

I open the door and face him. "How could they know I was coming here? I mean, to take the…the MacGuffin."

"I don't know. I can only guess that that agent of yours made you 'an offer you couldn't refuse.'" He adds, "That's a line from a new movie with Marlon Brando."

"*Last Tango in Paris?*"

"*The Godfather*. It's great. I saw it in New–" He stops himself. "You'd already left!"

I brush by him and go to the window, looking out at the awakening city of Tehran. "Glad you were having movie dates and a grand old time while you were fleeing dangerous assassins."

Sirens wail outside. There is a sharp cracking sound, like a distant shot.

I picture Monsieur Frochot, with his comically thick glasses and pencil mustache. The thought of him engaged in some kind of international smuggling is beyond ridiculous.

Harry leads me to the sofa. I don't even want to look at him. He lights a cigarette. "Look. I knew we were doing some shady stuff with the art – but I had no idea where the money was going. I mean, besides our pockets. I guess I just didn't care, and yes, I know, that makes me a bit of a prick –

"A bit?"

"—but it wasn't harming anyone. Here, for example. The rich Iranians want to get their assets out. The Shah's reign is getting shakier and the mullahs are widening their power base. The police are holding it together but there's a lot of resentment brewing."

The demonstration that was or wasn't a "riot" depending on who you asked. I decide not to mention it to Harry.

He continues, "What started as a profitable lark is now a tricky situation that will be sorted out forthwith." He's pale and his hand is unsteady as he tries to light another cigarette, forgetting he has one burning in the ashtray. "Oh, enough of all this! Can't we forget about it for now? I love you and I think you love me."

Do I? It isn't much use to insist you "shouldn't" love someone when it's already too late.

He takes my hand. "You're off for a few days, right? There's so much to see."

"What about the MacGuffin?"

"If you'll let me, I will take it off your hands, get it to the right person, and we can both forget about the stupid thing."

"Please."

Harry carefully rewraps it and puts it in his bag.

"How did you know I was in Iran?"

He grins. "I only just found out a few days ago. Nareem Mirsheid-aie's a client. And they had a dinner party. They'd invited this wonderful singer named Rebecca Bell. I was late. It broke my heart because I so wanted to surprise you."

Like a film fast-reversing in my head, I see the empty chair at the Mirsheidaie party, the limo racing past me as I'm leaving. Harry was there, and I just missed him. But now I've found him – well, he found me – and all the rest really doesn't matter.

21

$\mathcal{H}$arry plans an excursion for my two-day break. In a borrowed Peugeot – from a "pal" according to Harry – we leave the outskirts of Tehran behind and speed north toward the Caspian Sea.

"We're off-season, of course." He cranks up his window against the cold air. "But that has its good points. No tourists to speak of."

"We're tourists."

"Yes, but we're exceptionally classy tourists. Wish we could take the mountain road, it's gorgeous, but dangerous this time of year."

The alternate route winds through a tunnel blasted into the rock, higher and higher until we are over eight thousand feet up, clouds above and below. My ears pop. I wonder what the "dangerous" route would have been like. Harry pulls the car over at the highest peak and we get out of the car and stand near the precipice. The sea stretches out beyond the mountains, a rumpled gray blanket. Wind whips my hair into my face, and for a moment I'm dizzy from the height and a lack of sleep. Harry's hand grips my arm. The thought comes to me that I don't really know all that much about him. I shake off the feeling. His arm is around my waist as we gaze out at the spectacular view.

Bowl of Night

We stop at a tiny café overlooking the ocean below, all but obscured in mist. The cheerful, welcoming owner speaks little English, but Harry knows enough Farsi to order from a handwritten menu. The café is an extension of the owner's small house; salt air of the sea mingled with cooking spices. A goat grazes in an adjoining yard.

The café owner's wife brings out two dishes of fresh black Caspian caviar. We squeeze lime onto it and eat it by the spoonful. The tiny eggs burst delightfully in my mouth. The next course is a platter of mounded, saffron rice, topped with the local specialty, meat and vegetable kebabs. I let Harry eat the meat part. He downs a vodka and lime juice, while I settle for a glass of pomegranate nectar. Just when I am certain I can eat no more, we're presented with an outsized serving dish of sweets; plump, juicy dates, baklava dripping with honey, and small, baked nut cookies. A pot of freshly brewed tea completes the meal.

"The local tea farms are the best in the world," Harry says.

"Tea *farms*?" I picture trees with pots of tea hanging from heavy branches. "And are there scone ranches?"

"The wild scone is hard to tame and requires special scone wranglers." He drains his second vodka.

"Should you be driving?"

"You can drive if you like. Besides, we're not going much farther. Not by road at least." At my questioning expression, he adds, "It's a surprise."

The café owner's son, a boy of about ten, brings out crafts for sale. He explains in halting English that his mother makes the carved wooden bowls and plates. The work is intricate, designs burnt into the wood. I especially like one that has the image of a horse galloping.

"I guess you were one of those horse girls," Harry remarks.

"I wanted to be, but we moved around so much, I never had one of my own. I thought at one point I'd grow up to be a jockey, but I got too tall."

"And so you became a singer instead of a jockey. That follows."

"No, first I was going to be an astronomer, until I found out there is math involved. But I always sang. Hymns, of course. And more hymns."

"I only know a couple of hymns. 'How Great Thou Art.' I always thought 'How great thou, Art' and who was this bloke Art?"

While I'm laughing, he adds, "I always did like that Royal Navy one that goes, "O hear us when we cry to thee, for those in peril on the sea." His eyes fill. "I don't know why that one always gets to me. Perhaps it's a foreshadowing, that I'll die at sea."

We both gaze down at the ocean for a long moment.

"But I'll probably just die in a pub."

I swat his shoulder.

Harry negotiates with the Persian boy for the small wooden plate, agreeing on fifty rials, which is about a dollar. He hands the horse plate to me. "I'll buy you a horse. We'll live on a ranch in…how does California sound?"

The icy wind kicks up again. "Right now, pretty good."

It's warm inside the car. Harry briefly takes my hand and kisses it. He moves his hand to the shift, and we set off. The road curves along the seacoast, passing towns and villages with odd and exotic names. The Fodor's map shows Marzanabad, Babol, and Sari, which is thought to be the place where Indian saris originated in the Middle Ages, because of the region's rich silks.

We pull over again to take in the mountains draped in snow. The green of an early spring is already struggling to be born. A pomegranate tree with fruit like crimson and a white snow shawl.

"There are silk farms," Harry says.

"How do they teach the silkworms to sew?"

He takes me in his arms, and whispers, "I completely adore you."

The sea is a deep, fathomless blue. The mist lifts, and the sun bronzes the water.

He drives back to the main road and an offshoot that takes us inland again, but only for a few miles, off the paved road onto a dirt one that ends at a small airport. A dozen or so planes are parked in a field, most covered with protective tarps. Nearby there's a yellow biplane.

"You're not afraid of flying in a small plane, are you?" he asks.

"I was in a crop duster once." I haven't thought of this in years. "The pilot dropped pesticides on the cornfields. Then he tried to impress me by doing aerobatics, and I threw up and he got pissed off."

"Well, that's just a lovely story, isn't it?"

A man jogs across the field toward us. Harry claps him on the back. "My pal, Buck!" He introduces us. Buck has a broad, weathered face, and deadpan eyes. I wonder if he's ever smiled. Buck leads us to the yellow plane.

"Where are we going?"

"Just an aerial tour of the country!" Harry says, delighted. "No time to explore everything, so I thought this would be the best way to see it."

"Really?" This thing looks like it was patched up with silly putty.

"I…I wanted to surprise you." I've never seen him uncertain before. "I know, it's not exactly a Lear jet." He hugs me. "But it takes off, flies, and lands."

"Antonov-An-2," Buck says to Harry, ignoring me. He has an accent that is sort of Persian, but not quite. They talk about the engine, a Shvetsov something-or-other, built by Russians.

Harry helps me up a ladder into the plane. There are cracked black-leather seats for six passengers, and an empty space behind. A drab-green woolen blanket is folded on my seat and a headset rests on top. I slip it over my ears. It makes talking all but impossible. The plane races along the runway to the point I wonder whether we'll get off the ground before the runway ends. Fortunately, the plane wins. We ascend in bumps and dips, up over mountains that seem to grow taller as we rise, barely skirting the snow-capped peaks. Since the sun is low behind us we must be heading east. There is no heat, which explains the blanket. I wrap myself in it, up to my chin.

Harry turns in his seat and smiles, raising his eyebrows as if to say, *Isn't this fabulous?* He looks like a little boy who just got his first train set.

We swoop gracefully through a pass into canyons, and then down farther into a valley. Frowning, Harry taps Buck on the shoulder. No response.

The plane slows and banks lower, wind buffeting and bouncing us. I grip the arms of the seat. We're aiming for a long, flat spot between the hills that looks like a strip of masking tape. It seems improbable that the pilot can put the plane down in such a narrow space, but the wheels touch the ground gracefully. It jounces along the rugged dirt road, and stops near a group of mud-colored, low buildings, all but camouflaged in the shadows of the surrounding hills.

I stumble slightly when Harry helps me to the ground. My ears are still humming.

He shouts to Buck over the engine noise, "What the fuck is going on?"

The forsaken land stretches out. It is a place of extraordinary, desolate beauty, like the skin of the moon. The wind pulls tears from my eyes.

"Fuel," Buck says, and walks away. Harry stares after him, clearly unhappy.

"How do you know this guy?"

"He does some jobs for Alistair."

"Is there a problem?"

"No, no, nothing to worry about, I just wished he'd told me there was a stop." He points at a small Quonset hut nearby. "You can wait there. It's warm and there's probably some coffee or tea." So he's been here before. Harry trots down the dirt road after Buck.

Several olive-drab trucks are parked nearby along with a pair of military-type helicopters with Cyrillic writing on the sides. Is this some kind of army base? I spot a few men but they're not wearing uniforms. The Quonset is warm inside. Afternoon light, softened by high windows, gives the interior an opaque glow. Rugs cover some of the hard-packed dirt floor. A woman, all but invisible inside her chador, sits near a small stove. Electric wires snake out the back of the stove, extending to a noisy generator that also provides heat, in the form of three glowing space heaters.

There is a makeshift table and four paint-flaked Adirondack chairs, which look as if they might have once graced the lawn of a Cape Cod estate and are so out of place, I wonder if I'm hallucinating.

"Do you speak English?" I ask the woman.

She shakes her head. All I can see of her is a pair of large, dark eyes, and these seem very young. "Parlez-vous français?"

Apparently not.

I point to myself. "Rebecca." The woman nods. "Where are we, anyway?"

The impassive eyes gaze at me. The generator hums. I really have to pee. "Where is the bathroom? Toilette? Loo? Ladies room?"

"Loo!" she says. She points outside and to the right.

"It was nice talking to you."

No sign of Harry. I follow the dirt road, growing angrier with every step, and reach another building. By now, I really need to find a bathroom. The building has a creaky, half-opened door. Long, rectangular wooden crates are stacked to the ceiling, nailed shut, with numbers imprinted on the sides. I pass between the stacks of crates to the back of the storage area. More boxes fill the space, but these are smaller, and have what looks like Chinese letters. There is a girlie calendar on the wall, showing a beckoning Asian woman, nude save for a red Christmas bow on her pubic hair. At least someone had the holiday spirit. And here's a filthy toilet with a creaky door. I slip inside, trying not to touch anything. Fortunately, I have a wad of tissues in my bag. The sink runs cold water. There's a limp, dirty towel I don't go near, instead drying my hands with a few more tissues.

As I exit the disgusting loo, a man calls out in Farsi or Arabic. Concealed behind the crates, I can't be seen unless he walks down my row.

He goes still, listening, as if some primal sense has alerted him to my presence. Or perhaps he followed me. Why am I afraid? Harry is here. Buck is an employee of Alistair's. It's just a routine shipping place.

Right.

The man says something in a demanding tone. Seeing no other options, I step out. He's in the doorway, about fifteen feet away, a rugged workman in a cap, dirty jeans, and a brown windbreaker. He sees me and takes off his cap, in a respectful way. I say, "Loo," hoping that explains everything. He nods and steps back to let me pass through the door.

I spot Harry across the road, talking and gesticulating to one of the men, and I run towards him. I just want to get out of here. Harry takes my arm and we walk towards the plane.

"What is going on?" I whisper.

"Nothing. Just a misunderstanding. I thought this was going to be a joyride, but apparently Buck had an errand to take care of."

Harry is carrying a brown leather satchel.

"What's that? Part of the 'art business'?"

No reply.

"Everything about you is a lie, isn't it?"

"I love you. That's the truth, so help me god."

"And if you believed in god, I might take you at your word." I look around at this desolate place. It doesn't take a genius to work out that Alistair and Harry – and Buck – are all in the same business. Whatever that is. And maybe I'm in it, too.

"Beautiful, isn't it?" Harry says.

"In a forbidden fucking planet kind of way."

Buck is ready to go. The plane's engine growls into action. I take one more look around and perceive the movie of my life as a crane shot, retreating from our forms, which grow smaller in the lunar landscape until we are unrecognizable.

22

I thought we'd fly back to the airfield where we left the car, but Harry – or Buck – has other plans. I enjoy the flight, which lasts well over an hour. I once lived near an airport and I'd watch the planes swoop up, shrink to the size of toys, and vanish and wonder where they were going; what the people inside were doing; if they could see a girl lying in a field far below wishing she could trade places and fly away. When I was fourteen, Dad was invited to speak at a meeting of evangelicals. He took me along, perhaps hoping I'd meet some nice Pentecostal boy to marry. The flight from Kansas City to Denver was not even half full. The stewardesses were pretty and wore short skirts, which upset my father. I wanted their outfits. As it turned out, I did meet a boy, also the offspring of a preacher. We slipped off to make out while our dads were at meetings. He kissed with his mouth closed, seemed terribly uncomfortable, and, in hindsight, was probably gay. I never saw him again.

Buck puts the Antonov down in a small airport. A taxi is nearby. We drive towards a city. Through the taxi windows, I peer at the street names, similar to those in Tehran: Shah. Reza. Pahlavi. The ancient city is sprawling, urban, sophisticated, colorful; vastly different from the sheer primitiveness of where we just were.

"The Mongols and Turks and the Uzbeks used to raid this region for slaves," Harry tells me, as we drive past orderly traffic circles and wide avenues. "It's mostly peasants and farmers, and it's one of the holiest Shi'ite sites in the country."

Many of the people wear traditional attire; turbans and billowing robes for the men; headscarves and even full chadors for the women. Afghans are conspicuous in their distinctive flowing garments and long, loose headdresses.

"I thought the Shah outlawed those clothes."

"His father did, in the 1930s, but it's not as harsh as it was back then. Western dress is considered more upscale, more businesslike. But in the more conservative areas – holy cities like here – there is much more traditional dress. Mashhad is a pilgrimage site and the land is mostly controlled by the Imam." He points out an enormous mausoleum with a brilliant, gilded copper dome, flanked by two minarets. "That's their Jerusalem, their Vatican, the sacred city. The Shi'ite pilgrims come all year round."

Harry gazes out at the passing streets. Just seeing his profile makes me fall in love again and again, as if loving him is an infinite succession of waves. I love his knowledge, his humor. Even his unpredictability.

"What a remarkable part of the world this is," he says. "So old. And troubled. It's been one religion against the other since time began. Well, that's the whole world, isn't it? There's always some crackpot who starts to believe God is on his side."

I think of my family's all-encompassing piety. "There are some *good* religious people." Their narrow-mindedness, their lack of curiosity about the world. Guilt stabs me. They meant well.

"Of course, but it only takes one fanatic to corrupt the whole bunch. And religious movements attract those people."

"I grew up with so goddam much god, it becomes unreal, like saying the same word over and over until it loses its meaning."

I can see them, the children of god of my childhood; the seekers, the lost, the deluded, the desperate, under the tent. Rain hammering the canvas roof.

My brother became so obsessed with saving the unborn, they were more real to him than the living. I told him, from the perspective of my nascent feminism, that a woman should be able to decide about being pregnant. He looked at me with horror, his golden hair glistening in the sun like some avenging angel, and I backed up, afraid he would strike me. He turned away, and we never really spoke again. In a few months he would take his gun, stake out an abortion clinic in Missouri, and shoot, killing one of the doctors and wounding a patient. Gideon, a martyr to the cause.

"Those who think they have the answers are self-deluding fools," Harry is saying. I wonder what he would say if I began speaking in tongues. "And, to answer your earlier comment, no, I don't believe in a god that 'sees all, knows all.' I don't believe there's a god that takes sides in a war, or a sporting event, or a disaster. An 'act of god,' if you will. A couple of towns near here were wiped out a few years ago in an earthquake. Is god mad at them?"

"How the fuck should I know?"

"For a Sunday school girl, you've got quite a mouth on you."

"It comes from hanging out with musicians. And from being forbidden to say those words when I was growing up, or even hear them. Nothing makes you want to say the 'f' word more than not being allowed to."

"The forbidden fucking fruit."

"Speaking of, I'm hungry."

We pull up in front of a small hotel. It's difficult to believe that just a few hours ago, I was in a grubby warehouse in the desert. Within a few moments, we're in a cozy room, with a high double bed and down pillows.

I strip off my clothes and run the bath. An array of soaps and a small packet of bubble bath beckon. Although bubbles kind of creep me out. Something about clusters of things, like fly eyes. I smash them. On the other side of the door, Harry tries to make a phone call; I hear him arguing in English, then French. Immersed in the hot bath, pleasure floods my entire body. After a few minutes of blissful oblivion, I open my eyes and scan the room. The wallpaper is a pale floral. The sink has old-fashioned claw feet, and an arched, curved spigot polished to a high-gloss gold. The bathtub fixtures are the same, with a soap holder that slides forward along the sides of the tub.

I use my toes to shut off the faucet. With the water stopped, I hear Harry in the other room, "…not a problem…just get the stuff across and we'll…later…"

I lie absolutely still, so as not to stir even a ripple of water.

"…tomorrow morning, probably…"The rest is inaudible.

23

*W*hen I come out of the bathroom, Harry is in bed, stripped to his jockeys, with the leather satchel between his legs.

"Want to see what's in here?"

"Is it alive? Another McGuffin?"

"Ha." He up-ends the bag. Thick packets of U.S. bills tumble out. Hundred-dollar bills. He removes the rubber band from one and spreads out the cash like a deck of cards.

"Is it real?"

"I may be many things," he says, "but I haven't yet added counter-feiting to my resumé."

He takes the rubber bands off two packets, hands me one, and tosses his in the air. I do the same. The money rains down on us. We laugh and roll on top of it. The bills crackle under my back and stick to my bare skin. The sight, the tenderness of Harry, the sheer madness of that much cash is intoxicating. The world slows into microseconds of sexual heat, expanding exponentially until I am sure I can take no more. He brings me along slowly, using his hand and then his mouth, and when he finally moves over me and enters, I am desperate with want, the cash notes crushed limp with our sweat.

We order dinner in the room, but have to quickly gather up the piles of money before letting the waiter in with our meal. After we've polished off a bottle of wine, I doze off in Harry's arms, into a comatose sleep.

When I wake up, I have a moment of complete disorientation. What country? What city? Harry is already dressed, and stuffing the money back in the bag. There's about three hundred in Iranian rials on the dresser.

"Hey, I'm worth at least a thousand."

"A million."

"We only get to be rich for a night?"

"We're going to be a lot richer than this."

Once, I believed in flying horses. I drew the horses and the wings separately, cut them out and pasted the wings onto the horse's back. I ran around "flying" the horse, and several times dreamed that they were real, and I was flying over the farm fields and everyone looked up, shading their eyes and marveling.

Would we be rich, and together? Perhaps there are flying horses we haven't found yet.

"I have to meet someone. This is the last of all this bullshit." Harry closes the satchel. My Harry: always halfway out the door, blowing me a kiss, promising to return, and only occasionally keeping his word. He says, "I love you very much." A hesitation. "If I'm more than an hour, take a cab to the airport and get a flight back to Tehran. I'll see you there." And he's gone.

I can see gleaming gold minarets from the window and Harry getting into a taxi. He turns and waves at me.

I pace the room. Shower, dress, wait. An hour. Ninety minutes. That's it. I throw my few things into the overnight bag, and head to the lobby.

"Mrs. Lamb," the desk clerk calls out, looking at me. I realize that I'm Mrs. Lamb. "Will you be staying another night? Your husband only paid for the one night." He says this in broken English that takes me a moment to decipher.

"No. Sorry. I'm…we're checking out." I consider asking him to make a flight reservation for me, but it all just seems so complicated, and my head is throbbing.

A taxi is idling in front of the hotel. At least I have the little tourist phrase book stuffed in my purse. "Foroudgah, beformayd." Airport, please. The cab rushes through the streets. This city is almost as big as Tehran and just as crowded.

Iran Air has a flight out in an hour and an available seat.

I'm exhausted, and nod off sitting on a bench, awakened when the flight is announced in several languages. I follow the line to the tarmac, just as two soldiers approach, one tall, with a thick beard, the other stockier, his hair covered with a dark woolen cap. They carry Uzis.

"You come with us," the tall one says. The gun clanks against his belt buckle.

24

I t appears I will not be getting on that plane. What is incredible is how little attention my "arrest" draws among the people waiting to board. A few heads turn, but I get the feeling no one wants to see anything they might be asked about later. The two soldiers walk me through a door off the airport's main waiting area, past a nest of offices, and into a small room. Pale, dusty spaces on the walls and floor remain where furniture and shelves have been. There is a gray metal table, three chairs – one on one side, two on the other. On the wall hangs a large, framed photo of Shah Reza Pahlavi, dressed in royal robes and with a rather benign expression, as if it were important to him to be well-liked.

"I want to go to the American Embassy. Qonsolgari Amricay."

The taller soldier laughs. The other demands my passport. He grabs my purse and upends it onto the table. The contents spill out; lipsticks, tissues, Tampax, pens and pencils, a comb, my notebook, the Farsi phrase book, assorted pieces of paper, dust, and a nail clipper. And the passport, which they take. They let me scrape my possessions back into the bag and leave me alone in the room.

I'm shivering, even though it's not cold. I'm also sweating. How can a person do both at once? My mouth has gone dry and I am having trouble taking a breath.

The door opens and a different man enters, trailed by the two soldiers. He has a thick, dark mustache and is dressed in civilian clothes, clearly in charge.

"Good afternoon, Miss Bell," he says, in almost perfect English, offering his hand as if we are meeting for tea. After a cursory shake, he gets right to the point. "We are not in the habit of detaining Americans, especially young women, but yours is an unusual situation. However, I think we can clear up matters very quickly and send you on your way. You may even be able to make your plane to Tehran."

I try to reply but my voice won't work.

"Bring Miss Bell a glass of water," he orders the short soldier. "And, please, Miss Bell, sit down and be comfortable."

Reluctantly, I sit on the hard, wooden chair. There is writing scratched into the table, the same Arabic letters over and over; a cry for help or of madness.

"You were recently at a storage facility owned by an English businessman. I would like to know who brought you there and what you were doing."

"My…friend and I, we were on a short holiday. It was a fuel stop, that's what the pilot said. I don't even know where we were."

The muscles around the interrogator's eyes tighten. I notice he has a small black mole near his temple. *You should get that looked at,* I think of saying, *it could be cancer.* The absurdity of this nearly makes me laugh aloud. Dylan's "It Takes a Lot to Laugh, It Takes a Train to Cry" floats through my head, gets stuck on one phrase and plays on a loop.

The short soldier returns with the water, in a cloudy green glass. They might have slipped in a drug; I could be kidnapped into white slavery and perhaps Ellen was right when they were all joking about this back in Paris. I don't touch the water.

The man-in-charge dismisses the others.

Being alone with him is more frightening than the three men together. At first, he paces around the room, idly touching the chairs, the table. He draws his finger along the edge, over the scratched words as if he is reading Braille. He pauses in front of me, his body uncomfortably close, and since I am sitting, it is his groin that faces me. A faint mix of soap and flesh, cigarettes and sweat waft from his body. Bile pushes up into my throat. I swallow hard. Standing up is impossible; he is too close, and I would be forced to brush against him.

He lowers his voice. "Miss Bell, we know you were traveling with an Englishman calling himself Harry Lamb, and a Pakistani pilot. Mr. Lamb is your lover. We would very much like to talk to him but he seems to have left the area, although not with his pilot, who is right at this minute in one of our jail cells. They are not very nice places. If you know where Mr. Lamb has gone, I would appreciate it if you just tell me and not waste our time, or force me to take harsher measures."

I take a breath, surprised at how difficult this is. "I don't know where he is. That's the truth. He...he left me." I begin to cry. Tears had worked back in Missouri when a state trooper wanted to give me a ticket for speeding. And when a customer got hostile at a go-go bar, accusing me of bilking him for drinks (he was right), I turned on the waterworks. Not that I have a choice now. "He left me at the hotel and didn't tell me where he was going. I have barely enough money to get back to Tehran, and I spent it on the plane ticket."

"I understand your distress, Miss Bell," he says, unimpressed. "But please understand my position. I have a job to do. There are matters of national security. If you'll just tell me what you and Mr. Lamb were doing, then we can clear this up. We're not in the habit of imprisoning young American women, although it has been known to happen."

"Har – Mr. Lamb and I went on a short holiday," I repeat, "and then we flew to this other place. We weren't there long. Maybe an hour. I think it had something to do with Mr. Lamb's art business."

"Really. So this is some kind of art gallery in the desert. Or perhaps a museum?" He sweeps his hand across the table. My purse items scatter. The glass shatters against the wall, the water forming a rivulet that creeps toward my feet. I choke back a scream. In the deathly-still room, I hear the rough sound of my own breathing. An idea comes to me.

"I have friends in Tehran," I say, carefully. "Mr. Nareem Mirsheidaie. And his wife, Eleanor. We were going to visit them at their country estate, where they raise Arabian horses." Of course, I barely know the Iranian oil heir. But I sense, correctly as it turns out, that money is power here. As it is everywhere. The Mirsheidaies are loaded, and close friends of the Shah.

The officer examines his manicured nails, picking a smudge of dirt from his thumb. "Nareem Mirsheidaie is a very nice friend to have. I imagine you have a lot of gentleman *friends*."

"I have just enough."

"Do you know what I think?" He doesn't pause for an answer. "I think you are a stupid tourist who ought to go back to your home in America, get married, and have a lot of babies." He moves away from me and opens the door. A rush of air flows in. The two soldiers are outside.

"I may just do that," I say, with a note of defiance. I stand up, unsure if they will try to stop me. "May I go now?"

"One more thing," the officer says. "In Tehran, we have in custody a man named Omar Khash, who used to work as a comedian. He mentioned you when he was being questioned. Isn't that strange?"

A sick dread spreads through my bloodstream. "I don't think it's all that strange. We were performing at the same nightclub. Frankly, he was…uh, attracted to me, but I turned him down. I think this made him angry. So, I wouldn't trust anything he had to say about me."

The man-in-charge tosses my passport on the table and leaves the room as abruptly as he'd come in, with no parting words. I'm free to go. I gather my purse things from the dirty floor. There's still time to catch my flight.

25

The flight back to Tehran gets delayed, and I have barely enough time left to make my show on time at the Diamond Hotel. My hand grips the taxi's armrest, willing the cab to move faster. The sun has long since set in a molten meltdown I watched from the window of the Iran Airways plane.

I quickly shower and freshen up and then tune the guitar. It needs new strings. I'll have to find a music shop in the next few days. The soldiers and the interrogation room appear in my mind. I push the thoughts away, into the crowded cave of bad memories.

Hurrying down the hallway to the club, I nearly careen into Mr. Meskat.

"Miss Bell! I think you have not gotten my phone call!"

There was a red message light blinking in my room but I was too rushed to check.

"I'm not late."

"No, no, I'm sorry, this is so awkward, but we no longer need you to perform. We have a change of show." He shrugs, as if it were in the hands of the gods. "The owners demand a new program. I called to tell you but you were apparently away."

He is blocking the doorway to the dressing rooms, and avoids my gaze. "What?"

"Yes, yes, sorry, you are a very nice singer and I'm sure you will find much success back in France and America."

"Are you telling me I'm fired?"

"Fired? Oh, no, of course not. Your booking is at an end sooner than later, that is all."

I walk around the corner to the club's entrance, trailed by Meskat. My picture is no longer on the standing poster board. Valerie Marchand's is there. The comic who replaced Omar Khash. And a glossy photo of a tuxedo-clad magician, his hands stretched wide in a posed flourish, a willowy blonde assistant behind him, dressed like a belly dancer and holding a rabbit.

"You replaced me with a *magician*? And a *rabbit*?"

"He is a very fine magician, with many astounding sleights of the hand," Meskat looks personally insulted.

I storm back to the stage door, still shadowed by the club manager. "I need to get my things." I have very little in the dressing room. Some makeup, a few magazines, a guitar capo.

"Miss Bell, we have already been so kind as to pack your performance items, and secure them behind the front desk. Please ask the clerk, when you are checking out." He hands me an envelope.

"Checking out?"

He opens the stage door and disappears inside. I'm alone in the hallway, gripping the handle of my guitar case, fingernails digging tiny half-moons into my palm.

"Rebecca?" Valerie Marchand comes out of her dressing room. "What has happened? You are leaving?" She seems genuinely surprised.

"Yes. Something came up and I have to get back to Paris."

"I am sorry to hear this. You are so talented."

This is the first time Valerie has said something nice to me. Or much of anything. I assumed she thought I was some boring folksinger, if she gave me any thought at all. I turn away so she can't see me start to cry but she puts a fragrant arm around my shoulders. "Don't be concerned. I have been in this business for many years and there have been good experiences and bad, and so many stupid people! Those are the people who get to be in charge, of course." She laughs. "You will be fine. Wait here, I have the name of someone in Paris you should call." She goes back into her dressing room and a moment later comes out and hands me her card, with a name and number written on the back: Sylvie des Anges.

"Sylvie has the most popular nightclub in *le tout Paris!* Go to see her."

"I've heard of Chez Sylvie."

"C'est ma soeur." Her sister! "She knows *tout le monde!*" Everybody.

Valerie gives me a hug. "Bonne chance, ma jeune amie!"

In my room, I look in Meskat's envelope; a week's salary. But it's a check and I have no way to cash it tonight. Scathing, indignant remarks bang around in my head; everything I should have thought to say to everyone. Starting with Harry, the Rat. Anger replaces the fear that has eaten at me since that airport. Does my worthless French agent, Frochot, know about this? I pick up the phone to call him just as there is a sharp knock on the door.

A young hotel flunky stands in the hall. "Mademoiselle Bell, I am sorry but we have booked this room to another guest, and since you are no longer in the employ of this hotel, you are to please vacate the room."

"To*night?*"

"I am sorry, but am only following orders."

"Well, all right, you Nazi fuck, just give me time to pack."

"There is no need to have unpleasant language."

I slam the door in his face. This is the second time today I am being kicked out of a hotel. That must be some kind of record.

Everything goes into the suitcase wrinkled and squashed, clean and dirty, shoes and dresses commingled. I have to sit on the lid to close the suitcase, and feel the hinges give slightly.

I stride through the lobby to the front desk with as much dignity as

I can muster. The least they can do is book me a flight. The desk clerk is pleasant and seems unaware of my situation. He calls the airport, and asks about flights to Paris. "I'm sorry, Miss Bell, but there is nothing until tomorrow afternoon. Shall I book that one in your name? You will pay when you get to the airport."

"Yes. Yes, please. And can you cash a check for me?"

"I'm sorry, we cannot do that. You will have to go to a bank."

And, of course, since it's Friday night, nothing will be open until Monday. So much for paying for an airline ticket. "Um, never mind, I can call the airline later."

He looks apologetic. "Please, I will have someone help you with your luggage. Will you want a taxi?"

But where do I go? Another hotel? I used half of Harry's three hundred dollars to get to Tehran, and flying back to Paris will be more.

Well-dressed guests arrive, stepping out of limousines. They've come to see the show. *My* show. I look in my purse for an aspirin and find a few dusty pills at the bottom. And a slip of paper, with a hastily handwritten name and address: Trish.

For a second, the name means nothing. Then I remember the hippie girl in the market, who gave me hash and blathered on about astrology. She said to come by any time.

When the taxi pulls up, I have a destination.

26

As the taxi speeds toward the outskirts of the city, I pop two aspirins dry. The driver turns the car down a dark, unevenly paved street. There are no streetlights, and the only light is a crescent moon. A few candles flicker inside a clustered row of small, ramshackle homes. At the dead end of the street there is a larger house, and this is the address. I give the driver a handful of rials.

The house has flaking paint and an incongruous veranda, an afterthought that slants down on one side. It was probably once a nice place for a middle-class family. The steps creak and give. I move slowly, so as not to trip in the darkness. Pushing the bell elicits no sound from within, but I can hear music playing. I knock hard. The music stops. There's a murmur of voices and then the door opens a crack. A young guy with stringy black hair and dark eyes squints at me.

"I came to see Trish. We met a few weeks ago. She invited me."

"Trish!" he calls out.

The music resumes – "Martha My Dear" from the Beatles' *White Album* – and a woman appears in the doorway, dressed in low-slung jeans and an old T-shirt. She barely resembles the robed wraith from the bazaar, but I recognize the blue eyes and untamed tendrils of pale-blonde hair.

"Hey," she says.

"We met at the market."

"Yeah, I remember. Gemini, right?" She leads me into a living room/crash pad, randomly furnished with low-slung chairs and a few sleeping bags. The guy who answered the door returns to the sofa to watch a soccer game on an ancient black and white TV without the sound, while the record player provides a soundtrack. At the other end of the worn couch is the guy's double. They pass a hash pipe and offer it to me.

"Sorry, but I have a terrible headache. It's been one hell of a day. I wonder if I can…stay for the night. I lost my job. I can sleep on the floor, really it's no problem." I stop for a breath, but feel compelled to fill the silence. "I know it's an imposition, but if I could just stay here till I can get some money and a flight out."

"Sure," Trish says.

A sparkling migraine halo teases at the edge of my eyes and nausea fills my mouth. My head throbs with a drum inside.

"Are you hungry?" asks the twin who had answered the door. "I think we've still got some pilaf."

His voice seems to come from some distant realm. "I think I have to lie down." The light in the room, dim as it is, feels like a knife. I stagger back. The twins leap up and catch me before I fall.

Lying on a thin mattress on the bedroom floor, I drift in a haze of pain, and vomit into a wastebasket. Someone puts a cool damp cloth over my eyes.

In the morning, I'm limp with a migraine hangover. Trish makes pancakes, the aroma awakening my appetite.

The guy who answered the door is Lazarus; his twin brother is Peter. They grew up in Pittsburgh, dropped out of some small college, and to avoid the draft, drifted through Canada, where they met Trish, and an importer bringing merchandise out of Afghanistan. The money was good. The twins want to go back to America, once the Vietnam war is over – it has to end *some*day, right? – and figure they could slip back into the States through Canada.

We're all sitting at the kitchen table, drinking strong Turkish coffee out of small cups.

Trish reveals that she was part of a radical group in the U.S. "I blew up a building once." She pauses. "It was supposed to be empty, but there was a janitor."

"He *died?*"

"But they did weapons research. So…" She says it as if that makes up for the janitor. "It would be dicey for me to go back. To North America, that is. At least for a while."

"You'd go to prison?"

I've noticed that Trish has a way of telling embellished stories, so this could be just another one.

At night, I retreat to my bedroom early, weary from trying to be sociable. My hosts talk all the time; long, rambling, stoned dialogues. I turn down their offers of pot and hash and whatever, fearful they will bring on another headache. On my cot, I'm besieged with thoughts of Harry, a train wreck of colliding memories.

The twins are so indistinguishable, I just think of them as a unit called Peterus. At first I thought Trish was sleeping with one or both of them, but apparently they all tried each other out and lost interest. Friendship, Trish assures me, is a lot easier. Although, she adds, it's better to fuck the guy first to get that out of the way, so he doesn't always wonder about what he might have missed but can congratulate himself on having had you.

Two days slide by. Three. I need to call Frochot but it's like I'm catching the Trish/Peterus inertia. We collaborate on dinner, usually some kind of rice dish, augmented by whatever meat or fish or fruit Trish has scavenged or bartered from the bazaar that day. They are awaiting a delivery, one of the twins tells me, and then they'll have lots of money and we can all go out and celebrate. Had I been to any of the small music clubs? Maybe I could get another job singing? He plays the guitar, too, and thought he would be a rock star, but doesn't like the idea of 'selling out.' I let him play my guitar; he knows three chords, barely, and plays them over and over until I gently take the instrument away.

I tell them a little about myself, omitting the trip to the desert camp, and the figurine, and the police, and getting kicked out of the hotels.

Trish says, "There's always a guy."

I'm sitting outside on the lopsided porch when a woman passes by, stops, and says hello in Farsi: salaam. I return the greeting and that's the end of my ability to communicate in Farsi, so I ask her if she speaks English. Yes, a little. More than a little, it turns out. She – Yasmin – lives a few doors down, with her family. Parents, husband, two young children, a brother. They used to live in a nice part of the city but it's become too expensive. Her house is as run down as the one Trish and the twins are renting, and even smaller. I try to imagine seven people sharing the space.

The twins want to accompany me when I go out to find a payphone. The neighborhood is getting worse all the time, they tell me. No, I'm fine, I'll be careful. I don't want to insult them but I need some space. There's a phone in a shop about three blocks away.

Yeah, the area is a shithole. Shacks and houses close together. Filthy waterways run parallel to the road. The people wash their clothes and themselves in these fetid streams, and some even carry home water for cooking. Groups of small children follow me, curious. The Diamond International and the glittering streets around it seem like another planet.

Frochot is surprised to hear from me. "It is good at the nightclub?"

I update him, the same edited version I'd given to Trish and Peterus.

"That ees unforgivable!" he protests. "I will think again about sending a talent to that nightclub!"

I'm sure if the money were enough, he'd put aside his indignation.

"*D'accord*, I have some good news," he says. "There is a record company, a small French label that is interested in your songs. They want to produce English-speaking artists for the European market. I tell them about you, say you are at fabulous resort for several months. But you are returning soon? This ees much better, to 'jump on a bandwagon,' *non?*"

My mood leaps and fast-forwards to making the record, getting airplay, a top-forty hit, a ten-LP deal, a European tour, making the charts in America. Meanwhile, I'm living on the largesse of a trio of drug-dealing hippies. I don't share this with my agent.

"The club manager gave me a check I have to cash, and then I can get a flight. I don't have enough—"

"No, no, I will wire the money. Tell me where."

Where? Good question. "I don't know. Maybe American Express? Or the American Embassy?"

"Oui, the embassy is a good idea. I will send it right away. *Je suis désolé*!"

"I'm sorry, too."

27

Trish decides that a farewell Tarot card reading is in order. I have no interest but she's insistent, and hands me the deck to shuffle. "Think about what you want to learn from this. What is your question? You don't have to say it aloud."

Will I ever see Harry again? I give the deck back to Trish with my left hand, as instructed.

"Trish is really good at this," says Peterus.

One by one, Trish turns over the cards and arrays them on the floor, in a cross shape. Several of the cards are upside down. She places one in the lower right corner, and silently contemplates. Shifting expressions cross her face.

"What?"

"Well, this is interesting…"

"*What?*" Despite my skepticism, I want the cards to provide answers. Happy ones.

"This," Trish taps the card at the bottom, "is your past. The Tower." The illustration resembles a castle under siege. "You've left behind some old beliefs and found new freedoms, and it scares you but you'll eventually be stronger." She frowns and touches the card on the left, the Four of Cups upside down. "You're afraid of being left alone, of abandonment, losing love." She turns her attention to the card on the right. "Now this represents things working for you. The Knight of Swords. He's a good guy, but he comes and goes in your life."

"He's a good guy?"

"Kind of. But you can't really count on him."

"No shit."

The twins creep closer.

"Number four, on top, is the near future. The Page of Swords, reversed. He's connected to the Knight, but not in a good way. Deception, deception, deception. The card in the center is the long-term future. The Eight of Swords."

"Uh-oh," says Peterus.

"Don't say 'uh-oh,'" I tell him.

"It's not a good card," Trish concedes. "There's a lot of difficulty, but help is available. You just have to look for it in the right place. But this one is the outcome, and it's good." The card standing alone is The Wheel of Fortune. "See, even bad luck will turn. You may not understand your destiny now, but eventually, it will all become clear."

"Am I going on a long voyage?" I joke. The reading, vague as it is, gives me a jittery feeling.

"Yes."

"Where does it say that?"

"It doesn't, but you're going back to Paris, aren't you?" Trish laughs.

She turns over the last card: Death.

"Are you kidding me?"

"No, it's not what it appears. Yes, it can mean actual death, but more often it means a change, a rebirth."

"Or it could just mean death."

"Possibly."

"Mine?"

"Not necessarily."

Maybe the cards are the work of the devil, as my father would have maintained.

"When I was in London, I read Mick's cards." Trish's conversation is often peppered with names like "Mick" and "Jimi" and even "Elvis." Apparently, there isn't a rock star she hasn't met or fucked or hung out with. "The cards said he was going to die before he was thirty."

"Well, he'd better hurry up." The cards didn't even bother to answer my question. Did I really think they were magic? We always want to believe.

Trish passes a joint around, and mentions that the stash is getting low. Their last dealer, a local, nearly got arrested and has dropped from sight. And anyway, they need money.

"There's this guy from Afghanistan," says Peterus, "told me they're making a killing transporting poppies. You know, they turn the flowers into—"

"Heroin?" Trish laughs. "You think we're going to smuggle *heroin*? Are you nuts?"

"It's just an idea. Lotta money, fast. I ran into him at the, what is it?" he asks his brother.

"Rezabad Café," other Peterus fills in.

"Right. They got music there. I told the guy I'd meet him."

Trish interjects, "No fucking way. They're already watching us."

"You're just paranoid," he insists.

The other twin adds, "I really don't think they give a shit about any of us. And the guy probably won't even show up."

Trish pushes two pieces of bread into the rusty toaster.

"We could just feel him out, see if he's on the level. If it sounds too risky, then fuck it," Peterus replies. "And Rebecca could sing and pass the hat." He looks at me. "I mean, if that's okay."

"Sure. My room and board."

Two pieces of toast fly up into the air, startling all of us.

"Goddam piece of shit!" Trish pulls the toaster from the wall and tosses it out the window. Other Peterus retrieves it. His brother distracts Trish by asking her to read their cards, too.

We drive in their ancient, exhaust-spewing car to the Rezabad Café, a scruffy, smoke-filled hangout for students, Eurotrash expats, and Persian Europhiles. When we arrive, a man is sitting on a stool in the corner, banging out a Kurdish-inflected "Hey Jude" on his guitar. The proprietor welcomes us. The Peteruses introduce me and the guy is happy to have some American entertainment, especially when one of the twins adds that I played at the Diamond International and in Paris.

After I sing, Trish passes around an empty shoebox. We count up the equivalent of four dollars. The Afghan connection never shows up. But when we get back, there's a note from the guy, and the deal is on. There'll be a big payoff in a couple of days; all they have to do is hold the stuff until the guy's connection comes to take it away and gives them the money. I've observed that my hosts' sense of time is a little skewed. The transaction might take weeks.

In the morning, I take the bus downtown to collect my money at the American Embassy, a fairly modest building, with Persian tiles adorning the walls of the entrance kiosk, catching the light. The lobby is crowded with tourists. At the information counter, I wait on a long line, behind a woman with a sick, screaming child and an angry group from Ohio, whose hotel had turned out to be nonexistent. An hour later, the receptionist at the information desk sends me to the money exchange, where I wait another hour for my name to be called. I show my passport and am given an envelope containing four hundred dollars. There is a travel office where I'm able to make my plane reservation. I'll be leaving for Paris the next morning.

Night has fallen by the time the bus brakes in a cloud of dust, several blocks from the house. There had been no set route; the bus, packed with the city's service workers, stops whenever anyone wants to get off, and by the time I realize I'm near my destination, we're speeding past it. It's dark out; the moon a shadow behind clouds.

Bowl of Night

Two official-looking cars are parked in front of the house. The door is wide open. Down the street, a dog barks an unceasing no! no! no! Curtains are closed in the neighboring homes. I step behind a parked truck, hidden from view but able to see the house.

Two SAVAK burst out the front door, carrying a package. No, it's a person. I recognize one of the twins. His feet drag on the ground. The other twin walks out, prodded at gunpoint. His hands are trussed behind his back and he is crying dirt-streaked tears. The boys are tossed into the back of the first car.

Another policeman leads Trish out the door. She's cursing in English and Farsi. They shove her into the second car, as both vehicles squeal off into the night. The dog continues to bark.

A few neighbors venture out into the street, talking in low voices, and then go back inside. There isn't a breath of life on the pitch-dark street. Even the dog has stopped barking. I have to go in and get my belongings. But what if the cops come back? A half hour passes with no activity. Now? More time passes. Darkness. The bubbling sound of water trickling along the gutter. Lights go out, house by house, shack by shack. A baby cries. Now?

The door is open just as the police left it. My father used to have a joke. When is a door not a door? When it's a jar. "Daddy," I whisper. *Pray*, he tells me. *The Lord is my shepherd: I shall not want.* The porch creaks like a rifle shot *He maketh me to lie down in green pastures, he leadeth me beside the still waters* a noise like a sigh is the refrigerator motor kicking on *He restoreth my soul. He leadeth me in the paths of righteousness for his name's sake* the chaos of the living room, bookshelves torn from the walls, furniture ripped up and overturned *Yea, though I walk through the valley of the shadow of death, I will fear no evil* throwing my possessions into my suitcase, this! and this! where is the other shoe? leave it for Christ's sake! The guitar, yes, the guitar *for thou art with me, thy rod and staff they comfort me* where are the fucking car keys? *Thou preparest a table before me in the presence of mine* enemies: *thou anointeth my head with oil* the car keys on the table *my cup runneth over* I stumble over Peterus' guitar, the strings ringing in protest.

Miraculously, the car starts, rattling the silence *surely goodness and mercy shall follow me all the days of my life* the clutch makes a painful scraping sound when I try to put it into gear but we lurch forward, stop, start, forward again, and it's moving *and I will dwell in the house of the Lord forever...*

Driving fast to Mehrabad airport. The lights of the city are clearly visible in the north, and the airport is somewhere in that direction. I come to a wider road that leads to an expressway. Modern high-rises illuminate the skyline. Traffic speeds by on both sides, with only a casual regard for road rules. Drivers randomly swerve across lanes at high speeds. I grip the wheel, keep to the right, and let them pass me.

The poor old car gives a threatening rattle. I don't have a clue what kind of car this is. Don't fail, we're nearly there. There are road signs in Farsi, and under the lettering, the symbol of an airplane. I press the gas pedal and the vehicle shudders. As I near the air terminal, the car slows, coughs, but struggles on, passing under the soaring arch of the Shahyad monument at the entrance to the airport. It was built to celebrate the country's 2500th anniversary, just a few years ago.

I turn into a parking lot on the outskirts of the airport and pull into an empty spot. No one is around. I wait for several minutes, lights out, engine off. My suitcase and guitar are in the back seat, where I tossed them.

I abandon the old car and head on foot towards the brightly lit terminal about a half mile away. The guitar case bangs against my leg and the suitcase is leaden. Cars pass, a flock of taxis, honking their horns, gridlocking. Even at this late hour, the airport is as busy as any daytime hub. Mehrabad is centrally located, and flights come in from time zones all over the world, twenty-four hours a day. I am one of many entering the wide doors into the terminal. Lines of travelers crowd the counters.

The people between flights fill the benches, indifferent to the disarrayed woman with the musical instrument case and the vintage suitcase.

Three heavily armed SAVAK police stand guard. One notices me and quickly steps forward. I freeze.

"A guitar, right?" he says, grinning. "I like Elvis. 'You are nothing but a hot dog.'"

The airport clock says one AM. My flight is at eight in the morning. It's too early to check the luggage. I find an empty chair and settle into it, clutching my bags. After a while, I close my eyes.

It's nearly five when I wake up. I take my things with me into the ladies room. The stall barely contains me, the suitcase, and the guitar.

An Englishwoman is saying, "… they can get us on the earlier flight, apparently it's not full…" and someone responds, "Of course it's not full, they tried to blow up that plane in Iraq, who in his right mind wants to fly now?"

My next stop is the Air France desk. Yes, they have an earlier flight, two hours before the one I am booked on, but it isn't direct to Paris. It goes to Amsterdam and there is a layover, but yes, there have been cancellations and seats are available.

I'll take it.

They search the luggage. An official asks if I am bringing anything of value out of the country. I recall the day I arrived, the figurine tucked into my suitcase. Well, at least I'm rid of that thing. No gifts? He seems suspicious. No, I repeat. The other guard opens my suitcase, rifles through the mess of clothes, the evidence of haste and panic. He snaps the lid shut again. The suitcase is checked through, the guitar after it.

A procession of weary, rumpled travelers waits to board. A mix of Iranians, Arabs, Europeans, backpackers, businessmen with briefcases and distracted expressions. Women with cranky children. Everyone with too little sleep. The line creeps forward. I clutch my ticket in sweating hands. New soldiers have taken the place of the night shift. I feel as if a spotlight is picking me out of the crowd.

The flight crew secures the doors and settles in for takeoff, and the plane rolls down the tarmac. Beverages are served and breakfast – a baguette, jam, butter, eggs – just as if everything were normal. But my mind spins; Harry, Tehran, The Diamond Hotel, Omar Khash, the pilot, the place in the desert, money, sex, Trish, twins, police. It was all a really strange dream.

Except it wasn't.

Part III

28

"Good afternoon, Sleeping Beauty." Max Hurwitz backs through the doorway from the kitchen, bearing a tray with a pot of coffee, two cups, and a plate of croissants.

I'm on his sofa, the sheets twisted, slipping off. I called Max from Orly airport. He picked me up and brought me to his flat. The décor is an awkward mix of tastes; things left behind by the person from whom Max sublet the place, and his own hodgepodge of possessions, books, papers, record albums, guitar, all permeated with a faint musty bachelor aroma.

Max sits next to me on the couch. "I suppose you'll fill me in eventually," he says. "About Tehran."

"Oh, it was just your ordinary pleasure trip." I pour coffee like it's liquid salvation. Grab a chocolate croissant.

"Do you want some music?"

"Sure."

He selects a James Taylor album and the song fills the room's empty spaces. "Fire and Rain."

"What's wrong?" Max asks, noting my stricken expression.

"Nothing. I mean, I'm just really really tired." I devour the croissant, and take another. "How is Ellen? And Jimmy?"

"Ellen moved into a new flat. Jimmy went home to Hong Kong for a couple of weeks, and he just got back."

Max opens the blinds to a gray afternoon. Even though the apartment's heat pumps up through audible steam pipes, I feel a chill that sneaks in under the windowsill. Max moves around the room, picking up a book here, a magazine there. The pocket of his plaid flannel shirt is torn. His brown corduroy jacket is draped over an armchair, a chair pebbled with tufts from a cat's claws. There is no sign of any cats. I wonder if I could ever love a man who wears baggy corduroy, if he could save me, if I will ever belong anywhere.

I pour another cup of coffee. "Does April in Paris ever really happen?"

"Ha! Give it a week or two, and then all the flowers will bloom at once."

There's a pre-snow stillness in the air, as if the city were already muted. Snow is rare in Paris. I want to be snowbound in this warm, safe flat. As if on cue, a few random flakes float past the window and quickly thicken. When I was a small child, the snow and rain caused me to worry about stray animals. Will they freeze? I asked my mother. No, they're smart enough to find shelter. And their fur coats keep them warm. Yes, but what about their feet?

There's a creak in the hall. The door is locked, the chain pulled across. No one knows where I am.

"…is a convenient excuse for not finishing anything, and then she just goes on to the next," Max is saying.

"What?" I've lost track of the conversation. Something about Ellen? I start folding up the sheets, replacing the sofa bolsters. There is the usual handful of loose change, a bobby pin, a pen. "I really need a shower."

"Right in there. Towels in the cabinet below the sink."

The water is so hot I nearly scald myself, and I have to juggle the hot and cold to get the right balance. My toothbrush is still in my unpacked suitcase, so I use his. I wrap myself in Max's terry robe, which is hanging on the back of the door.

Max is settled on the cat-clawed chair, regarding me. His fingers interlock like a church steeple, touching his chin. With glasses he looks very academic. I realize I don't know much about him.

"You were a lawyer, right? What kind?"

"The boring kind. A lot less interesting life than yours."

"Oh, right, traveling all over in a Christian cult is real exotic."

"Nice Jewish boy. Brooklyn. Law school. Disillusion. Freedom – although that turned out to be a myth. Like the myth of being a Paris expatriate. I keep missing all the exciting times. The '68 student riots. Woodstock. I'm like the Lost Boy in *Peter Pan* who's always out of the action and when he comes back, they're sweeping up the blood."

"As long as the blood isn't yours."

"Yes, that can be a plus."

The music on the stereo now is Crosby, Stills and Nash. *Our house...*

"I can probably get a room at the Hotel Paradis again."

"You can stay here as long as you like."

"You're a gentleman, Max Hurwitz."

"That's the burden I carry. While the bad boys get the girl."

"Not always." I run my hand along his arm. He faces me, his feelings in plain sight. We kiss, a friendly, exploratory kind of kiss.

"You don't owe me anything, Rebecca."

"Shut up," I kiss him more deeply, to see if I can feel anything.

He pulls away. "I never thought I'd hear myself say this, but I don't think this is the right time. You're too lovely, I'm too lonely, and I think you love someone else."

"I look like shit. No wonder you're not interested."

"You know that's not it." He touches my shoulder. "What's going on? Are you in some kind of trouble?"

I spill it all out. Well, some of it. From meeting Alistair Nelson in London and getting the figurine, to Trish and the twins' arrest, leaving out the details about Harry, making him sound more like a casual friend. Max listens without speaking until I finish.

"You should tell someone about those kids getting arrested, or at least get in touch with their families."

"I don't even know their last names."

"Iranian prisons are hellholes." He pours himself another cup of coffee. "You certainly have an amazing instinct for being at the wrong place at the wrong time. And the figurine. Who did you say the artist is?"

"Zand Bahador. So lyrical."

"I'll check it out at the library, maybe I can turn up something that will at least explain why everyone is so interested in that thing. But you don't have it anymore, right?"

"Right. I gave it to…another art dealer. He said he'd take care of it."

"Good. Then that's done."

"Did you ever hear of a MacGuffin?"

"A what? Oh, you mean like Alfred Hitchcock's term? Why?"

Apparently everyone knows what it means but me. "No reason, just something I recently learned about." The snow has already turned to rain. Snow is only nice for about an hour. "I just remembered something. I met this woman at a dinner party in Tehran. She's a diplomat or something, at the Iran embassy here."

"Well then, that's a start."

"But I can't think of her name!"

"Maybe it's MacGuffin."

For dinner, Max makes scrambled eggs. I put together a salad. We share a baguette and a bottle of red table wine and watch television like an old married couple. The show is *Columbo*, dubbed in French. Later, Max translates the news for me. There is nothing about Americans arrested in Iran.

"I know! That diplomat woman. Her name reminded me of an old folk song. But I've forgotten which one."

Max pulls out his guitar. He starts playing "Michael, Row Your Boat Ashore."

"No, a woman's name."

"Could it be her last name?"

"No. First." I'm drawing a blank.

He strums and sings, "Oh, Susanna!"

"Nope."

"Eleanor Rigby? Oooh, Donna? Sweet Caroline?"

"No, no, old folk song."

He sings, in an exaggerated drawl, "In a canyon, in a cavern, excavatin' for a mine, lived a miner, forty-niner and his daughter, Clementine!"

"Holy shit, that's it! Clementine! You're a genius!"

"Are people really named Clementine in the twentieth century?"

"Well, this one is."

A cry comes from outside. I startle, heart pounding. "Did you hear that?"

"Hear what?"

"Someone screaming." But there is only the slow sludge of car tires on the melting spring snow.

Max puts a hand on my shoulder. "I have some Valium, do you want one?"

"Yes."

He goes to the cabinet over the sink, and brings back a pill and a small glass of water.

We watch TV until the sedative moves in like a fog. Max covers me with a blanket and turns off the television and the light.

29

Tucked away on a small street where Boulevard St. Germain intersects with Rue de Four is Club Sylvie, the très chic, everyone-who-is-anyone night hub named for its iconic owner, Sylvie des Anges. It's unprepossessing on the outside. This is the kind of place that doesn't bother to advertise its name or address because if you don't know where it is, well then, you probably shouldn't be here.

And yet here I am.

I've come late because it is a notorious after-hours destination, so I assume that by arriving at eleven PM I will find the club packed. The door guardian, a slim black man, looks me over. "Êtes-vous sur la liste?" He is holding "la liste" on a clipboard.

"Je suis un amie de Valerie Marchand, soeur de Madame des Anges."

"Américaine!" he says. It's difficult to tell whether this is a good or bad thing, but he waves me through the door. Dance music throbs in the mostly empty club. It has the expectant vibe of a room that is holding its breath. The high ceiling reflects a silver and crystal revolving ball. Discotheque is the new rage, a way for "white people to look good dancing" as someone quipped. I go directly to the bar, a long, silver and black affair, like mercury on tar, with recessed lighting. The club is all black, silver, and red, the banquettes crimson with black tablecloths, the walls all three colors, decorated with large modern paintings of the Warhol variety and dozens of celebrity photos. Sylvie with Mick and Bianca, Mick and Jerry, Mick and Jane Birkin, Brigitte Bardot, Elizabeth Taylor and Richard Burton, Halston, Salvador Dali, Jacques Brel, Elton John. The beautiful and the more beautiful. The famous and the infamous.

"Allo." A man takes the bar stool next to me, slim and angular, all Tartar cheekbones and tight black suit. Shoes that cost more than a Tehran-Paris flight. Rather gorgeous. There are the usual questions; name, nationality, the quick switch to English upon hearing my French, the "your first time here?" and the compliments. I play it cool and indifferent because the alternative is to act like a star-struck tourist. He's enjoying my tales of the Diamond International, and my validation from Sylvie's sister.

"Valerie is the older one," he tells me. "Ran away with a prince, got dumped, and washed up in the hotel circuit. Sweet lady but no taste in men."

Apparently, Valerie and I had more in common than I knew.

He buys me another drink. People are drifting in. The room fills quickly, more and more arriving, blowing in on air kisses, clad in Chanel and Yves St. Laurent, and very soon the designer himself is one of the guests, with his entourage of lissome mannequins.

Sylvie des Anges makes her entrance, working the crowd from dance floor to banquettes to bar. Her gaze sweeps over me and to my friend, Jean-Claude, who turns out to be Someone, I don't know what or who exactly, just one of the party people gifted in self-glamorization, and I am grateful for his voluntary patronage, not sure of his sexuality, and hoping he is as gay as gay can be so I won't have to fend him off.

"Sylvie! Meet my friend Rebecca! Chanteuse extraordinaire!" Of course, he has no way of knowing if I have any talent; my sole credential is Valerie and he has to take my word for that, but Jean-Claude, I surmise, is an intuitive type of social animal.

Sylvie offers a hand weighted by thick gold and diamond rings, bracelets as wide as my wrist. Her mouth is a slash of crimson under an untamed nest of vermillion curls; her eyes lined in black kohl. She is Colette come back to life, painted in the brilliant hues of a Mark Rothko canvas. Her hand is cool and thin boned under the jewelry. She sizes me up – No One, just a passing acquaintance of Poor Valerie throwing her life away down among the savages.

She and Jean-Claude embrace, speak rapidly in French, laugh. I might as well be a painting on the wall, only a lot less collectible. Sylvie glances at me again, for more than a second this time, and I must have something that intrigues her, because she grabs my hand and leads me on a serpentine journey of recognition and admiration from her friends and fans and the sycophants and superstars filling the dance floor, all the way to a back table where a small party is crowded in. She introduces me as "notre nouvelle chanteuse magnifique!" which seems a bit of a leap to me. Sylvie probably figures that no one will ever have to actually hear me sing, so calling me a great singer is hardly a risk.

I recognize Serge Gainsbourg, who made that wonderfully dirty record, "Je t'aime, moi non plus," with Jane Birkin, in which she moaned orgasmically throughout. Acting it out was a popular backstage pastime at *Au Naturel!* I immediately share this with them. Although *Au Naturel!* failed in Paris, it nevertheless carries a certain cachet of daring sensuality. In its brief heyday, it was *the* show to see on Broadway. The problem with the show in Paris, it seems, was that the nudity was hardly ground-breaking in a city of longstanding girlie glamour clubs like Crazy Horse, dating back to the late nineteenth century's Moulin Rouge. But the mere mention of *Au Naturel!* is enough to swivel the attention in my direction.

There are a handful of questions that the actors in *Au Naturel!* have heard hundreds of times. Here in the most sophisticated corner of the chicest city on the planet, nothing has changed.

"What was it like being nude on stage?" asks a stunning model with an Italian accent.

"Didn't you get cold?" her date says, with a laugh.

"It was fun. It was a show so there was a lot to think about besides being nude, and we did wear costumes in most of the sketches and no, we didn't get cold because there were stage lights, although it could be a bit breezy backstage."

"Did the men, you know, get aroused?" This, inevitably, from a man.

"We could be pretty mean. They didn't like to go out on stage with it in full…glory, so we'd rub up against them before we went on, and then they'd have to think about baseball or dead puppies to get it back down again."

Everyone bursts out laughing.

"Oh," says a petite redhead, "and what did you do when you, you know, had…" She lowers her voice. "Les règles?"

"What?"

The female guests offer an array of international translations: Aunt Flow. The curse. Shark week. On the rag.

"Got it." There's no way to put this politely. "We used Tampax and cut the string. It could be a bitch getting it out again."

The table erupts with screams of laughter.

"Oh that is so clever! I must do that with a tiny bikini!"

The women begin to share period stories. The men look stunned.

"Did you fuck a lot backstage?" A tall, rangy Englishman with a red silk ascot interrupts the women.

"Yes."

More delighted squeals.

"I shared a dressing room with two other actresses. One of them was involved with an actor in the cast, and they would go at it every night before the show. I would be putting on my makeup and see them in the mirror giving each other head." I pause for the reactions. "But I don't want you to think I'm some kind of a slut."

The young waiter, who had arrived with a tray full of new drinks, is standing by the table, gaping.

Serge waves at him. The kid comes out of his stupor and puts the drinks down in front of the wrong people. We switch them around. I end up with a martini I didn't order, but it's pretty good. I look at the men at the table and in the rest of the heated room shimmering with gorgeousness, both male and female, and wonder if I should go home with one of them and fuck Harry out of my mind.

"Rebecca?" It's the tall Englishman. "Would you like to dance?"

Will he be the one? Another Brit? We get up on the dance floor and flail around. The martini is hitting and the room is so hot I am disconnected, spinning, dancing like I am possessed. It's an exorcism. He grabs me around the waist and spins me in a circle. His aftershave is pleasant but wrong, and feel his large, strong hands gripping my sides. One dance song blends into another, and I don't know how long we've been dancing. The strobe lights turn people into stick figures. I don't ever want to stop but he is tiring and wanting to get me alone, and then we are back at the table. Some places are empty, they are on the dance floor or leaving, and I have no idea how much time has passed. He is getting my coat from…somewhere…and we are out on the street on a crisp early spring night, getting into a taxi, and arriving at an elegant building in, I don't know where, but his arms are around me inside the elevator cage. I can tell, even in my drunken state, that the flat is spectacular; wide windows looking out at the Champs Élysées, which means we must be in the First? Big bed with white coverlet, and all I can think about is fucking Harry on the pile of money.

30

I stumble back to Max's flat early in the morning, wretched from too much to drink, not enough sleep, and the leaden guilt of the bad girl. I remember just enough of the night to know I didn't feel anything but emptiness.

Max has left me a note that he's gone to class and maybe I can meet him at the Alliance and we could go to dinner nearby. I kill half the day sleeping, then take a bag of my dirty laundry to the *laverie* down the block.

There is the glitter of Sylvie's. And there is the oh-so-ordinary world of the Alliance Française. Regret wells up in my head. I should have taken classes here, learned the language, stayed in Paris, forgotten about Harry, said no to Iran. I envy the students milling in the hallways, gathering in the common rooms, and jabbering in French and English, Spanish, Italian, Japanese, wherever they find common ground.

The list of should-haves goes on; stayed in Missouri, not gone to New York, walked away when Harry Lamb materialized in front of me. Prayed more.

Even though the day is mild, I'm shivering, and wonder if I might be running a fever. My mother used to say that when you tremble it means the devil is walking over your grave. The devil is in everyday life, lurking, waiting for a slip-up and then he'll carry off your soul to eternal damnation. Evil may not be literal and pitchfork-wielding. *Satan will come in disguise*, my father said, but there is always hope. There is the Rapture, when Jesus returns to earth and the sinners and unbelievers are cast down into Hell, while people like us – the Bells and our disciples – yes, we would be saved. Everyone else…well, tough shit.

As a child, I believed this absolutely, but as I grew into adolescence and questioned everything my parents had ever taught me, I cast off their beliefs like woolen clothes on a hot day, while my brother dug deeper into the well of faith – blind faith – and, ironically, it was he who met the devil.

"…*je suis grand….tu es grand….il est grand….*," a class recites.

I will do it, I promise myself. I'll sign up for a beginner French class today. Or tomorrow.

Max comes down the hall. "You got my note, good." He kisses me on both cheeks. "Let's go eat. Ellen's meeting us."

"She must be thrilled that I'm back."

Max smiles. "Ellen may seem gruff, but she admires you. Jimmy'll be there, too."

"Well, at least someone will be glad to see me."

"Don't I count? I'm always glad to see you. Oh, and by the way, I found out a few interesting things about your figurine. Well, not the thing itself, but the artist. Zand Bahador. Seems he's some disgraced Persian artiste from the 1920s, and most of his stuff was destroyed or lost."

"Then it was valuable after all?"

Max shakes his head. "No, not really, that's the funny thing. It's basically worthless as a work of art but it's become some kind of icon of resistance movements around that part of the world. Anyone who feels disenfranchised by the powers that be, the West, the rich, you name it, well, they identify with poor Zand Bahador, who was executed by the first Pahlavi Shah in 1926."

Why would Alistair have it? To pay someone off? To keep someone quiet?

We enter Le Café, one of myriad small, shabby, wonderful restaurants that cater to students and the working class. Ellen Margolis and Jimmy Chen are already at a table, with a carafe of red house wine between them and a couple of extra glasses. Jimmy wears a black scarf wrapped around his head, like a ninja, and a Grateful Dead T-shirt. The look is a curious contrast with his earnest baby face.

Ellen holds out the *International Herald Tribune*. "Isn't it amazing?" she says. "They legalized a*bor*tion!"

"Who did?" I take a seat.

"America! It happened in January but I've been so out of touch."

"Same here." I'm confused about abortion. It seems like killing but it also seems like salvation.

"Well, then, let's drink to reproductive freedom," says Max, pouring wine for both of us.

"My brother was one of the anti-abortion activists," I blurt out. "He killed someone. A doctor he thought was doing abortions."

Ellen looks at me as if I've landed from another planet.

Gideon considered me one of the Lost when I went to the Big City, center of wickedness and sin, Jews and feminists. He warned me: beware. That was before he began to write zealous letters to organizations that were trying to get abortion legalized or that supported women's rights and civil rights, and to businesses that had Jewish names – he got this wrong more than once, harassing some German shop-owner in Kansas, who, as it turned out, was not terribly fond of Jews either.

Gideon's journey from innocence to obsession began on a stifling hot summer Sunday morning. In the middle of a service, eleven-year-old Gideon's eyes rolled up in his head and he began speaking in tongues. "Slain in the spirit, casting out sins," Daddy cried out, taking his re-birthed son in his arms and praising the Lord.

"Blessed assurance, Jesus is mine," we sang. I felt the ground under my bare knees, the spikes of dry Midwestern prairie grass pressing marks into my skin, and wondered when my turn would come, when God would speak through me and what was wrong with me that he chose Gideon instead.

Twelve years later, I flew from New York to Denver to see Gideon in prison. My seatmate on the flight was a forthcoming, sad woman whose thirty-one-year-old son had just died of leukemia. "I'm going to see my brother," I told the woman. "He's in jail." Of course, the woman wanted to know what he did to get himself locked up and as the words were coming out of my mouth – "he killed someone" – I realized that it can be a mistake to tell the truth to strangers or even friends. Like now. But it's out and there's no taking it back.

Gideon's trial was still several months away, so he was in county jail, not the maximum-security state penitentiary where he ended up. Still, the sign-in process for visitors was laborious; I had to provide I.D. and wasn't allowed to take any items into the visiting area, which meant I had to store my purse and return plane ticket in the trunk of the rental car. The waiting room had a row of attached orange plastic chairs secured to the floor. Nothing to read or eat or look at besides the posted list of rules on the wall about all the things one isn't allowed to bring in or wear, which included wallets, purses, pens, pencils, weapons, reading material, "revealing clothing," and bras with wires. I stole covert glimpses at the other people, wondering who they had come to visit and what crimes their friends or relatives or spouses had committed. No one spoke, or only in whispers, as if they were guilty of something, too. A uniformed guard leaned against a wall, smoking one cigarette after another. If Gideon had been drafted, I mused, had he gone to Vietnam, he would have had an officially-sanctioned enemy to kill. But childhood rheumatic fever had weakened his heart and he was rejected by the military.

The visiting area was television-familiar – a gray, concrete-walled room with a sealed, thick-glass partition between visitor and inmate, and narrow metal ledges on both sides of the partition on which to rest your elbows while cradling the receiver of a phone attached to the wall by a short cable. The only seat was a metal stool welded to the floor.

Gideon shuffled in, clad in gray prison overalls, smiling at first, pretending everything was just fine and this is where he needed to be to do the Lord's work. But he was pale and nervous, repeatedly slicking back his unkempt blond hair. A prison guard stood nearby.

"I haven't had any physical contact with another human being for three months," Gideon told me. "Isn't that weird?"

I tried to grasp the many ways this kind of sensory deprivation wore away your humanness. The rain Gideon would probably never again feel on his skin, the delights of plunging into the ocean, a simple, loving embrace. Well, he deserved it for taking a life. Yet, looking into his eyes, I saw only the boy who had been my annoying, silly, lovable little brother Giddy.

"Look." He extended his arms, bare and thin within the loose prison shirt. "The hair is falling out. Lack of sunlight. Like a mole."

When he was twelve, he sang "Amazing Grace" and brought everyone to tears.

"I'll get the gas chamber, you know," he boasted. His expression narrowed. "When they should be thanking me. They don't get it, do they, Becca? But Jesus knows the truth and God the Father will cast that wretched soul to the fires of hell while the protector of the innocents will be exalted to God's throne." Gideon's voice rose.

The guard stiffened, his attention now fixed on the prisoner.

I tried to draw him away from his obsession, by talking about my singing, my life, but each time he pulled it back – why am I not singing hymns, but mingling with sinners, homosexuals, and Jews? No one in the old congregation had been to visit. "Can you believe it? I am doing their work and now they cast me out."

"They never told you to kill anyone."

"They told me to do what's right."

"He wasn't even an abortionist. You shot the wrong fucking doctor."

Gideon studied the whitish skin on his wrists, the thin scars from a suicide attempt when he was fifteen. "That's what they'd like you to think. I know the truth even if they've got you and everyone else fooled. There's a whole movement to make it legal. *Make killing babies legal.*"

When he woke up on the morning that changed his life forever, did he know what he was going to do? When he left the house, the gun in his jacket pocket, did the weight of it make him feel holy?

As the visit ended, I realized I hadn't said half the things that had run through my mind on the plane; memories of our childhood, the time Mama and Papa accidentally left him at a gas station – he crawled out of the car, unseen, while I slept in the back seat. Many miles down the road, I woke up and asked, "Where's Giddy?" and they raced back to find him sitting on the curb, placidly waiting. There were long, glorious nights of singing, Gideon harmonizing in his pure, sweet tenor, on the old Bill Monroe bluegrass gospel tunes.

I would never get to say these things to him, although I didn't know it at the time.

Gideon was sentenced to death. Two weeks later, Colorado put a moratorium on capital punishment and later commuted all the death sentences, including Gideon's.

"What happened to him?" Ellen asks. My friends are horrified, as I knew they'd be, but I feel disloyal to Gideon, who was so much more than the dark act that came to define him.

"He hanged himself in his cell."

Nobody says anything.

Talking about it has made me lightheaded. Not to mention ruining everyone's good time. The bare facts, spoken out loud, do not seem to connect the brother I once loved with the murderer he became.

"Fanaticism," Ellen sighs. "Fundamentalism. It can sneak in anywhere, any country, even the so-called enlightened ones."

"Well," Max lifts his glass again. "To more enlightened times in America and everywhere else. And to the end of this fucking war."

We finish the carafe and order another, along with big plates of food. When my meal arrives, I realize I'm not hungry.

Max says, "You should eat."

"I know."

Ellen says, "I thought you were supposed to be staying longer in Iran."

"The whole gig got screwed up. They'd double-booked, can you believe it? At least they paid me and apologized a lot and promised to have me back." The lies flow right out. "Not that I'm all that anxious to *go* back."

"Was it bad?" Jimmy Chen asks.

"No, no, not bad at all. Tehran is amazing, so modern. The hotel is gorgeous. *Huge.* And my room was fantastic. And the club is big, too. But I felt, I don't know, lost, like I should have had a flashier act, or big band arrangements."

Ellen tucks a strand of frizzy curls behind her ear. "You need to sing in a small, intimate room. Don't get all *down* on yourself for not being Ethel fucking *Mer*man."

I'm taken off guard by this sudden empathy from Ellen.

"Excuse me." I push away from the table and flee to the bathroom. The cracked, silvered mirror reflects my misery. I wipe away the tears but the heavy feeling remains.

Back at the table. "Sorry. I'm still pretty jetlagged."

Jimmy puts his hand on mine. "If you need any help, you can call me. I don't have classes this week."

"Actually, things are looking up. My agent said there's a record company that's really interested."

Ellen's smile drops. Some people only like you when you're in some kind of distress. "When *I* was singing in New York," she holds forth, "they were *always* after me to go more belty and glitzy but I knew I just had to be my*self*. And anyway, I knew I wanted to devote more time to my *painting*."

Ellen singing in New York? Max and I share a look; *don't even ask.*

The waiter brings the check and we each scrounge up the appropriate change, with Ellen pretending she can't figure out her portion, and Jimmy throwing in the difference, even though we all know Ellen is a trust-fund baby.

Max and I walk back to his place. We stroll up Raspail, and along rue de Rennes toward St. Germain. I remember the man who'd once followed me, threatening and demanding I turn over the "little snake."

"I'm going to Spain for a week," Max tells me as we near his block. "A friend of mine rented a place in Malaga – but now I wish I could stick around here. Will you be okay?"

"Of course! It's warm there, I guess." He's going to ask me to come along, I think, and then I realize that his "friend" is a woman.

We climb the three flights to Max's place. "Funny," he says, "I don't remember leaving the door—"

"NO! Don't touch it!" I cry out, pulling him back from the threshold.

"What's the matter?" he demands. I'm already down the stairs, my long coat streaming out behind me. Max follows. "It's all right! It's the super, I forgot I called him about the radiator. He has the key."

The super comes out, apologizing. The radiator is fixed, he lets us know.

The apartment is too warm. Max turns down the radiator.

"Oh, shit, I am such a mess."

He adjusts the heat. "You need rest, we'll watch TV, you'll sleep…"

"I can't take your bed again. I'll sleep on the couch."

"Don't be silly, I can sleep standing up."

"You snore."

"So, I've been told. Look, I'll cancel my trip. I can't leave you like this."

"No, no! Go to Spain, for heaven's sake. I'll be fine after I get some sleep."

For this one night all I have to do is rest in the sanctuary of Max's home, messy and transitory as it is.

31

The Iran Consulate is on a quiet street in the 16th Arrondissement. My appointment is with Clementine Solis, the envoy – or consul or attaché or spy – who remembered me when I got her on the phone and mentioned the dinner in Tehran. I don't wait long before I'm ushered into her office on the second floor by her secretary.

"What brings you here, Rebecca?" Clementine, dressed in a black Chanel suit, gets up from behind her wide mahogany desk and beckons me to the sofa. "Would you like coffee? Or tea?" She's as striking as I remembered, the kind of willowy chic that this city seems to produce, and which I also saw a lot of in Tehran.

"Coffee would be great. Thanks."

She buzzes and asks in French for two coffees. "I must tell you how much I enjoyed your singing that evening. Did you like Tehran? I suppose you were too busy to see much of the country."

"Oh, I saw a lot more of it than I expected."

"That's good. It's a beautiful country, isn't it? Ancient and exotic and modern, too."

"Yes."

After an awkward pause, Clementine says, "You've come about some Americans in Iran? This is a matter of urgency?"

"Uh… I met these people, sort of hippies, I guess, and they might have gotten into some trouble with some drugs."

Clementine frowns. "And?"

"And…" The secretary comes through the door bearing a tray with a pot of coffee, cups, and milk and sets it all on the glass coffee table in front of us. There is a small plate of madeleines and a flower in a thin white vase.

Once the secretary has disappeared, Clementine pours the coffee for both of us. "You were saying about your friends and drugs. I'm sorry to say that this is not an unusual situation in that region. The young Americans seem to believe they're invulnerable. It's not the case, of course. If something happened to your friends, their families will have to take it up with the government. There's little I can do but make a few inquiries. What are their names?"

"There were twins, Peter and Lazarus. They're from Pittsburgh. And a woman, Trish. She's Canadian."

"No last names?"

I close my eyes, trying to remember. "Peter and Lazarus…. Bolton? Or Burton. The twins. And Trish…I'm really not sure. I'm sorry."

Clementine offers a sympathetic smile. "I can see you mean well, that you want to help your friends." She turns her palms out with a helpless shrug. "Someone will have to be looking for them. But I'll see what I can find out. I'll check with the American and Canadian embassies."

"Thank you."

She sips her coffee. "Are you in Paris long? Are you singing?"

"I'm kind of…looking for the right venue. And I'll be doing some recording."

"That's wonderful! I will buy your record."

Clementine's phone rings. "Excuse me." She moves to her desk to pick up the call. As she listens to the caller, whose voice I can faintly hear, scraping through the receiver, the expression on her face subtly changes, like the temperature has just dropped a degree. When she hangs up, she removes a thin, dark cigarette from a silver case and flicks a matching lighter. She regards me with curiosity, much like a cat homing in on a mouse.

I put my coffee cup down and stand, reaching for my coat and bag. "I won't keep you from your work."

"No hurry, dear. Enjoy your coffee. We can get to know each other a bit better."

I sink down to the sofa again.

"I heard something disturbing and hope we can clear the matter up before you go." Clementine puts on her Dior reading glasses and opens a file cabinet, removing some papers. "I want to be completely honest with you as I hope you will be with me. There is a reason I agreed to meet with you so quickly. In fact, I tried to contact you in Tehran, but you had already left the country. You were acquainted with Christopher Fargate, the art gallery owner?"

How does she know this? "Well, I *met* him a few times."

"He died, but you probably know that."

"A heart attack?"

Clementine's lips twitch with a hint of amusement. "When you were…with Mr. Fargate, did you ever meet any of his acquaintances?"

I stiffen. "I wasn't 'with' him in any particular sense. I just met him a few times. An art dealer in London gave me his name. We went out for a drink. Chris…Mr. Fargate gave me the name of a booking agent. Who got me the job in Tehran."

"I didn't mean to insinuate anything," Clementine says. "By the way, what kind of visa do you have?"

"I'm just a tourist."

"Yet you've been looking for work."

"Looking. Not finding. I figure that if anyone wants to hire me, I'll apply for whatever it is I'm supposed to get."

Clementine smiles. At least her mouth does. "I'm not trying to give you a hard time, dear. I'll be frank. There's a lot that this Fargate was involved in that was not completely legal." She laughs at what is clearly an understatement. "If he involved you in any way, it would be better if you tell me about it, before the French police or the Iranians get involved, if you catch my drift."

Why did I come here? I have a flare of anger at Max for convincing me this would be a good idea. But, really, I have no one to blame but myself.

The phone rings again. Clementine hesitates, then picks up the receiver. "I'll have to ring you back." She buzzes the secretary. "Hold my calls." She comes back to the sofa. I instinctively edge away.

"Sorry. Where were we?" Clementine gives me that half-face smile.

"I have no idea."

"Here's my dilemma. An item was brought into this country and then taken to Iran. The person who delivered it perhaps had no idea what the object was, or its significance, but that doesn't mean that the... the smuggler, for lack of a better word, isn't accountable. If you know anything about this, it would be helpful if you tell me now."

"I don't know what you're talking about."

Clementine sighs. "All right, why don't I tell *you* what happened, and you can correct me if I'm wrong. The art dealer in London gave you a small sculpture and asked you to deliver it to Christopher Fargate, who suggested that since you were going to Iran, you could bring it with you. Am I right?"

I see no point in trying to keep up the façade. "Okay. Yes. But I had no idea it was worth anything. If it *is* worth anything."

"And then you passed it along?" Clementine lights another cigarette.

I take a breath. "I think I was supposed to give it to a comedian working at the hotel. A *comic*! He said he was the one. But it sounded so ridiculous. And then suddenly he's gone."

She's still as a sphinx. "You still have it?"

"No!" Stalling, I take a sip of the lukewarm coffee. "Someone stole it from my hotel room."

"I see."

"Maybe it was the comic, Omar Khash? What happened to him?"

"Likely locked away, and telling them whatever they want to hear."

I flinch, the queasy memory of my brief experience with the Iranian police flashing back. "SAVAK arrested my friends – the ones I told you about – they dragged them away! The police...they're the bad people."

"There are a lot of bad people."

She's being motherly again. The old folksong runs through my head: *You are lost and gone forever, dreadful sorry, Clementine.*

"We don't really care about your little trinket. It's the path it takes that interests us."

I hear Harry's voice in my head: *I'll take it off your hands, get it to the right person...*

Clementine continues, "No one here has any illusions about the current government of Iran. But we believe it's the lesser of two evils."

Evil is evil. Isn't it? I rest my head in my hands. "Should I have a lawyer or something?"

"You're not being charged with anything. But you could be helpful. Can you understand that?"

"Don't talk to me like I'm stupid."

"I don't think you're at all stupid. In fact, I recall the way you held your own at the Mirsheidaies' dinner party, with all those envoys and diplomats. Your self-possession was impressive."

"Well thanks for the flattery and political science lesson, I think I'll be going now." I rise to my feet.

"Please. Don't go yet." Clementine stands up so abruptly she knocks an object off the coffee table; a small globe bounces on the carpet toward my feet. I pick it up and feel the cool glass in the palm of my hand. Inside the globe, snow swirls madly over a Paris skyline. I hand it to Clementine.

Her voice is low. "A lot of Iranians want the Shah gone. The merchants – the bazaari despise the royal government. They're the ones with the closest ties to the Islamic extremists. They hate the West. You've heard of Black September?"

"Of course. The terrorists who killed the Israeli athletes."

"They also assassinated Jordan's prime minister and were responsible for several plane hijackings and bombings. They would also like to see the Shah of Iran deposed or killed, so that the religious fanatics can come into power and support their cause. And there are people who are making things worse."

Her gaze bores into me as if she is taking a mental x-ray of my soul. I wonder if she's a good person or a bad person, if there is such a thing as good and bad, or if we are all just a hodgepodge of sin and salvation. We're supposed to strive for goodness. Be like Jesus. *Turn from evil and do good; seek peace and pursue it.* Assuming you can tell the difference.

As if reading my thoughts, Clementine says, "In every crisis, there are those who try to exploit it for their own ends. And it's the job of some of us to try to stop them." She gets up from the sofa and goes to her desk, opens a drawer and takes out a file, spreading out its contents, mostly photos, and beckons me over. I sit in the chair opposite, like I'm there for a job interview. She takes out a photo and pushes it across, facing me. I recognize him immediately.

"That's Alistair Nelson." Another photo. Christopher Fargate. I look at Clementine. "Okay…so…? She turns over another picture. The subject, a tall man with sandy hair, in a gray, belted raincoat. The photo was taken from some fifteen or twenty feet away, but he's unmistakable, standing on a busy street, looking into the distance, as if waiting for a bus or a person. I feel as if all the breath has been sucked out of me.

"You know him."

I can barely get the words out. "I…we've met." The window in Clementine's office faces a scaffolded building. I wonder if a person could scale the scaffolding down to the street, if a person wanted to escape. "What do you want from me, anyway?"

"We want this man. Harry Lamb. Your 'friend.'" She pokes her fore-finger on the photo.

"Why?"

"Why?" More photographs. Bombed buildings. Dead, mangled bodies. Men, women, children, limbs missing. Blood running. "What are these?" I don't even want to touch the rest. "Who are these people?" Another photo; a truckload of weapons. Another; Soldiers in black posing with the weapons next to more dead bodies, some of them children.

"Money changes hands. It's laundered through the quick sale of art works, antiquities, and other 'collectibles.' It turns into weapons—"

The crates in the desert. Quonset huts, trucks, boxes.

"—and the arms sales go to the bad guys, and the bad guys murder innocent people."

"Why are you showing me this? Yes, I know Harry Lamb! So what? He buys and sells art. Paintings! Beautiful things! Things that have nothing to do with all of…of *this*." I push the pictures back across the desk.

Clementine's eyes narrow. "Beautiful things?'" She turns another photo face up, and another, a deck of cards from hell. Each one is another scene of devastation. "This is what your art dealer friends are buying and selling. Death."

I leap to my feet. "You're lying! I don't know why but you are! Harry is kind. He would never be part of something like this. Not knowingly."

Clementine sighs. "I've been in love, too. It's your whole world. For a while." She carefully collects the photos and returns them to the file.

"I don't even know where he is!"

"Rebecca. I'm not going to threaten you or force you to do anything you don't want to do. But if you should change your mind… Maybe he'll contact you. Alistair Nelson is a good place to start. He's coming to Paris for the auctions. He stays at the Ritz. It would be easy for you to meet with him." She hands me her card. "Think about it."

I have to steady myself before I can walk out the door.

32

Max had tidied up before he left. The dining table, his "horizontal filing system," is cleared of clutter, save for a note propped up by a small, worn book.

> *Rebecca,*
>
> *I think you'll find this book interesting, to say the least. I've marked the page.*
>
> *Please feel free to eat everything in the refrigerator. I should be back in a week. Don't yet have a phone number but I'll try to call from Barcelona and maybe catch you between dangerous adventures.*
>
> *Take care of yourself.*
>
> *Max*

I leaf through the book, noting the publishing date: 1948, London. The title is the unrevealing *Folk Tales of Modern Persia.* The inside page shows that it was originally published by a Persian press, and later translated into English. I turn to the page Max bookmarked, but I can't focus.

The day is warm and perfect, and yet I'm shivering. Dizzy and nauseated. Am I coming down with the flu? No. The pain is much deeper, as if a hole has opened up in my chest.

I stuff the book in my bag and run down the stairs. But go where? A café? A bar? I head in the direction of the Alliance Française, but there is no reason to go there, so I veer right, towards Luxembourg Gardens. I should call Monsieur Frochot and ask if he's set up my recording session. I should do many things, but none of them will take away the images etched in my brain cells of those photo horrors, and the thought that Harry, my Harry, could be involved.

But why should I believe her? Clementine Solis, she of the Mona Lisa smile that seems to contradict itself. She doesn't know him but I do. And what about Alistair? He's the mastermind, isn't he, pulling the strings? Harry told me he'd gotten into something he didn't anticipate, and was getting out. Maybe I should meet Alistair, as Clementine suggested. He's behind all this.

At a café, there's a phone booth in the back. At first, I intend to call Frochot but a new idea jumps into my mind. The phone token slips from my sweating hand and falls to the floor. The floor is so dirty I don't want to pick it up so I try another token. My mouth goes dry as the number rings on the other end, and I'm tempted to just hang up and forget the whole thing.

"Nelson Gallery."

I give my name and wait for Alistair. For a moment I'm expecting the receptionist to come back on with a lame excuse. But he picks up.

"Rebecca! How lovely to hear from you again!"

I have a wave of déjà vu. "Alistair! I just wanted to thank you for getting me started in Paris, and for everything it led to!"

"It was my pleasure!"

I haven't come across this much bullshit since I stayed on a farm at age twelve. "And you'll be in Paris for the spring auctions, I'm guessing.

We should get together for a drink, and I can tell you all about my adventures. Especially with the little Zand Bahador piece that you so kindly entrusted to me." Silence on the other end. "And you'll be at the Ritz, of course, as always?"

An audible breath. "Of course."

"Well, then, what's a good time? I'm so looking forward to telling you about my travels in Iran. With Harry Lamb."

He coughs. "Sorry, a bit of a lingering cold." Another cough. "So you caught up with our Harry! Yes, I am interested in hearing about your… adventures. Let me check my calendar." Pages rustling. "How is next Wednesday? A drink? It will have to be late…"

"I'm a night owl. Your hotel?"

"Uh, no, I'll be across town, a favorite place in Les Halles. One of the few remaining. It's called Le Corbeau Noir. The Black Crow. I don't have the address—"

"No problem, I'll find it."

"Is eleven too late?"

"Not at all. I'm looking forward to it." I hang up before he replies.

My next call is to Clementine. I start to dial, and then quickly hang up. I owe her nothing. I want to see Alistair for myself and get some answers. Maybe I'll pass it along to Clementine; maybe I won't.

Outside the phone booth, an impatient male tourist, replete with neck-hanging camera and American baseball cap, is glaring at me. I drop another coin into the phone box and call Frochot, telling him I'll be at his office in an hour.

At the counter, I order a glass of red wine and a crepe, and find a sidewalk table. It's still late afternoon, with a bright sun casting a glow on pedestrians, cars, busses. I pull Max's library book from my purse, as the waiter brings my wine, and read the title again. *Folk Tales of Modern Persia*. The book is musty like attics and old trunks. I open it at the bookmark and begin to read.

The Story of Bahador

Wait. Bahador? Is this a biography? A true story or a fairy tale? Does it matter?

Early one summer morning in 1926, in a small Persian village, the artisan known as Zand Bahador shaped and cast into life a new sculpture; your humble narrator. I was – and still am – a small figurine that is not quite a dragon nor reptile nor cat but a little of each.

Neither the artist nor I, his creation, could possibly know that within a very short time, all that we loved would be in ruins.

Bahador's studio was a mud-floor room attached to the main cottage. After losing his wife in the influenza outbreak of 1918, Bahador, left to raise their daughter alone, could not bear to live in the city anymore, and so he abandoned their spacious, modern apartment, his friends and colleagues, and the urbane artist's life for a rural, dusty village just outside Tehran. Visitors came, some to buy, some just to browse without buying – to the annoyance of the artist, who was always was in need of money.

I held a place of honor in the studio and drew many admirers, particularly his daughter's, Parishad – whose name aptly meant "happy angel" - a sweet girl of fourteen, who often held me in her warm hands. Those were lovely days, the silky Persian sunlight slipping through the windows and under the door and throwing its beams on my many friends; the Granite Horse, the Lady and her Son, and the Leaping Fish. At night, after the artist and his daughter retired for the night, we played and sang. The Leaping Fish splashed in invisible water. The Granite Horse galloped. The Lady and her Son strolled a sunny courtyard. Along the walls, the beautiful Persian miniature paintings illuminated from within. By dawn we had each returned to our normal appearance, with the tacit agreement that the nights' secrets should remain so.

When Bahador was asked to create a garden sculpture for the new shah's birthday, he rejoiced that his money troubles would finally be over. There would be lamb for dinner and delicious fruits and sweets. His plans raced on; fix the roof and the broken floor tiles, and purchase the finest marble and new tools for his work and silks for Parishad.

One day, a representative of the Shah visited Bahador's cottage to discuss the commissioned work, the fee, and the deadline for delivery. Hesam was a tall, olive-complexioned man of Arab-Persian ancestry. He had served in the military and helped Reza Khan, who had been war minister and later prime minister, overthrow Ahmad Shah, and was then crowned Reza Shah Pahlavi. Thus, the Pahlavi dynasty rose to power and Hesam rode its coattails.

Hesam had a superficial knowledge of art. He moved about the studio, perusing Bahador's work, feigning expertise, and touching various sculptures and figurines on the shelves and the floor, until he got to my row and picked me up in his large hand, turning me this way and that. I admit that while his touch was a bit rough, I did not at first perceive the emptiness inside this man, nor anticipate the disaster he would bring to the household.

Interesting, Hesam murmured. What is it?

Just a bauble for my daughter, the artist replied. It is not for sale.

Disappointed, Hesam placed me back on the shelf. The emissary's attention was drawn to the outside, where Parishad was working in the garden. At that moment, in that fleeting glimpse, a fire ignited deep in Hesam's body, for here was a beautiful innocent and like many men of power – or with proximity to power, which is often far worse - Hesam was used to having things his own way.

He asked Bahador if he could court Parishad, but the artist, who had never recovered from the loss of his wife, couldn't bear the thought of giving up his daughter. She is young, he told Hesam. Come back in two years. This did not sit at all well with Hesam; his own sisters had been married off at fourteen, and his mother was barely in her teens when she wed his father. Hesam's personal ambition had taken him from the darkest poverty to the right hand of the Shah, and no inconsequential stone carver was going to keep him from his prize.

You should be honored to give your daughter to a high-ranking officer, Hesam pressured Bahador, but the artist was not persuaded. Hesam returned to his perusal of the sculptor's work, and came to the little Arabian horse. He said, I think something like this would be perfect for the Shah, slightly larger, although not life-size. His majesty is quite fond of horses.

Bahador concurred, and they discussed the price and how long it would require to create from black marble this beautiful Arabian horse. He would need at least a month. Hesam agreed, and promised that half the payment for the new statue would be forthcoming and the rest to be paid upon delivery to the palace.

Hesam got into his automobile – a shiny tan and black Packard sedan - for the drive back to the city—

"Mademoiselle? Crepe marrons?" The waiter puts the plate down in front of me, chestnut cream oozing out of the fresh crepe. I fall in love again with Paris at the first bite. And open the book to continue the strange story of the sculptor.

Bahador worked on the Shah's gift for weeks, trying and abandoning several ideas. Finally, the graceful Arabian emerged from the black marble.

When it was finished, polished to a high gloss, the sculptor wrapped his creation in cloths and placed it, wrapped in a goatskin sack, in his donkey cart. Bahador left at dawn for what would be a nearly three-hour journey to the palace, all the while imagining the wonderful reception he would receive; the congratulations of the Shah himself, the affirmations of Bahador's brilliance as an artist! But the city was noisier and busier than he remembered, the bazaars swarming. His exile to the country had rendered him more sensitive to noise and crowds, and he was eager to drop off the work, collect his money, and return home to the sanctity of the studio. There was no Shah to greet him – in fact, the young monarch was out of the country. Even Hesam was unavailable. Bahador turned his creation over to a secretary, who thanked him and wrote out a receipt.

On that very same day, Hesam had awakened with an increasingly familiar, carnal desire for the beautiful young Parishad Bahador. His resentment grew – why should he not be allowed to pursue the girl? A mere craftsman's daughter? He resolved to drive out to the artist's house and see her again. He found Parishad alone. She explained that her father had gone into the city to bring the commissioned work to the palace. Hesam was surprised and annoyed; he'd planned to be there when the work was presented, so that he could take credit for its creation. The wretched sculptor had cheated him of this moment of glory.

Parishad knew that it was improper for her to entertain a man alone. She asked the visitor to return when her father would be there. He assured her that this was business and her father would not want to lose a commission, would he? So, being a polite and well-raised girl, she offered the visitor tea and honey cakes, which he gladly accepted. She set their plates down on the cottage's wooden table and poured the tea.

Bahador's work filled every shelf and space in the cottage. Hesam found the presence of myriad creations, human and fantastical, to be disturbing yet strangely erotic and he became lost in a sensory haze, falling, falling into a longing he had never before experienced. He reached across the table and stroked Parishad's hand. His mind and body had already taken several leaps forward. Parishad tried not to show her apprehension. She stood up and went into the studio. At least there she had the pretense of showing the visitor more of her father's artwork. Hesam followed, close enough to grab a lock of her hair and pull her back toward him. He put his hand over her mouth and pressed hard, to make her understand that he would have no problem suffocating her or breaking her neck. Parishad went limp with fear. Hesam pushed her to the floor.

I watched all this from my shelf, helpless and mute. My friends also saw the violence and I will swear to this day that a tear rolled down the stone face of the Lady.

I stop reading, tears rolling down my face as they did on the stone and marble. Who are you and how can the figurine be telling the story? This must be some literary device I'm not familiar with. I push my empty plate away, and drink the rest of the wine.

The waiter appears, with a carafe. "Plus du vin?"

"Non, merci, l'addition, s'il vous plaît ." Quite proud of my French asking for the check.

I consider taking a taxi to Frochot's office, but the Metro will give me time to read more of the tale. Jardins du Luxembourg station to Châtelet to George V. As soon as I find a seat in the train, I take out the book.

Bahador returned at dusk. Even before he alighted from the mule cart, he sensed that something was wrong. There was not even a candle flickering in the cottage and the studio door was ajar. He ran in, crying out Parishad's name, and found her on the studio's mud floor, her clothes ripped and soiled, her face and body a mass of bruises from her defiler's fists. Her life's blood soaked the floor. Father, I'm sorry, she whispered, as if this were her own fault.

Who? he demanded.

Hesam, she whispered, with her final breath.

Bahador pulled his daughter to him as if he could will the life back into her body. If only he'd been there, but no, he'd had to deliver his work to the Shah while dreaming of the praise he'd receive! His hubris had caused his daughter's ravishment and death. Rage and pain collided in his heart. He rose to his feet and turned to the shelves and walls and floor filled with his creations. One by one, he flung us to the ground. Some were fragile and shattered in an instant while others were made of stone, and while they could not break, the ferocity of their maker's rage killed their spirits. But he saved his greatest wrath for me, Parishad's favorite. With all his strength, he hurled me through the window. I sailed up and up until I struck the rocks some two hundred feet beyond the cottage, rolled and rolled, and finally landed in a dusty patch of weeds.

Bahador set fire to the cottage and studio. All my beloved friends perished in the conflagration.

The artist—

I nearly miss my stop to change trains for the short hop to Georges V, and have to pay attention – not get lost in reading. A few minutes later, I'm at Frochot's office on the Champs-Élysées. He's alone, surprised and pleased to see me but less so when my first question is:

"Why did you send me to Tehran? Of all the places in the world?"

Behind the fishbowl glasses, his eyes dart back and forth. "Comment?" He's taken aback. "I thought was wonderful gig!" He pronounces it "geeg."

"Christopher Fargate didn't tell you to send me to Tehran?"

He sinks down into his copious chair, looking like a trapped animal behind his desk. "No, no, why would he do that?"

"Oh, never mind." Interrogating this little man is a waste of time. "What about my recording session? Is it booked yet?"

"I call you but you are not at Hotel Paradis!"

I jot down Max's phone number and pass it over. "You can reach me here for now."

"The recording ees next Monday. Ees okay?"

"Ees okay." My softening tone and a smile pacify him.

"Here is z'address of recording studio. Ten in the morning. You are ok to get up so early?"

"I'll manage."

After leaving Frochot, I stop at another café, order a cappuccino, and read the remainder of the story.

The artist returned to the city with a long knife concealed under his jacket. When he reached the palace, the guards recognized him from his earlier visit and allowed him to enter. He asked where he could find Hesam and was directed down a long hall to a small office. Hesam knew immediately that his deed had been discovered and tried to reach for the pistol he kept in his desk. He was too slow. Bahador plunged his knife into the heart of the rapist and murderer.

He gave himself up to the guards, who took him away to a prison deep beneath the palace. A month later, without fanfare or publicity, Bahador the sculptor was hanged; his works of art banned from the palace and the city.

Only I remained, a small figurine that was not quite a dragon or reptile or cat but a little of each, lying abandoned in a patch of weeds, waiting, waiting for someone to find me and hold me again.

The name of Zand Bahador and his artwork disappeared as completely as sand in sand. Time passed, and nature placed layer upon layer over me. I abided, quiescent.

The little village grew into a busy suburb, which required electrical power and plumbing, sewers, and transportation. A railway line passed close by. War came. It seemed that everyone wanted my country's oil and its allegiance. Britain and Russia invaded us;

the Russians from the northwest and the British across the Iraqi frontier. Reza Shah abdicated in favor of his son, who ascended the throne as Mohammad Reza Shah Pahlavi.

Persia – now called Iran - declared war on Germany and was rewarded with an invitation to join the United Nations. The great leaders Roosevelt, Churchill, and Stalin met in Tehran to plan the future of the war and what would happen after, when they divided the spoils. Iran, it seemed, would fare very well. Such prestige for such a small country! And all they wanted was...our oil!

That same year, on the outskirts of Tehran, a British Army squad began construction of an underground bunker. I heard the digging and the pounding and knew that my liberation was forthcoming. A hand reached down into the dirt. What's this? said a crisp English voice. I was hauled out of my sleepy grave. There was so much dirt and sand in my eyes that I couldn't at first make out his features, but he quickly dusted and polished me off and we took a good long look at one another. He was a very young man with reddish-blond hair, gray eyes, and a thin mustache. He stuffed me in the pocket of his fatigue jacket and continued his work.

Thus began my travels, for soon the second lieutenant was promoted and reassigned to Palestine and then sent home to London, where he opened an art gallery. I was relegated to a back shelf, and then a box in a closed room. I never saw my country again, except in dreams when I fly, soaring high up above the earth. Sometimes I catch a glimpse of the past in the silver spaces where time takes a breath before speeding on.

And then you came to me. To Harry. To the unknown. I try to convince myself that this is just a story, written by a person, and that works of art don't narrate, or think, or talk. Or love.

33

"*R*ebecca, ma belle chanteuse!" Sylvie embraces me in a whirl of Chanel #5. I'm here at midnight, falling headlong into the safe zone of my transient popularity. *Jungle Fever* throbs over the packed dance floor. There is nothing to do but merge into the dance orgy and let the music sweep me into its primitive heat. Seconds later, I'm dancing with the *Last Tango in Paris* actress, or her lookalike, clad in a red crepe, wide-leg jumpsuit and matching vintage cloche hat. I really need a new wardrobe.

The music, the volume, the sheer sweaty energy from a few hundred people are nearly enough to drown out my thoughts of Clementine, Harry, Alistair, and the poignant story of the ill-fated sculptor, Zand Bahador.

When the song ends, a man grabs my hand and pulls me to his table and I recognize a few faces from previous visits; the ones who loved my *Au Naturel!* tales of backstage sexual excess. Soon it will be too late to use this as an entrée; it will be a bit sad, like carrying around one's yellowing clippings. But not yet.

A new face is here tonight, a popular, blond-maned, model-handsome singer named Patrick Juvet, who's had string of hits. In his honor the DJ is blasting his bouncy "La Musica," already as ubiquitous as "La

Neige Tombe Sur la Mer." The tablemates chat in French, with the occasional apologetic glance at me or a perfunctory translation. Patrick Juvet says something about a song contest and Jean-Claude Muller, a short, wiry composer who has written for several pop artists, suggests I enter and there is a consensus that this is a wonderful idea, although it would require actually making a recording. Which, I tell them, is exactly what I will be doing the following week. Their plans for me race forward without my having to say a word.

The music segues into "Will It Go Round in Circles," and Jean-Claude beckons me to the dance floor. We try to shout over the music, but it proves impossible, so he smiles and shrugs and I close my eyes and surrender to Billy Preston.

With an abrupt change of pace, the DJ turns to Jacques Brel's heart-rending "Ne Me Quitte Pas." *Don't leave me*, the lyrics plead. We sit down and drink.

One of Jean-Claude's lady friends grabs a table napkin as the tears flow. She says, "Il est malade," eliciting shock among the guests, when she explains that the revered Jacques Brel is ill and could possibly leave this earth.

It occurs to me, and I don't know why it never has before, that Sylvie's is the kind of hip, upscale nightspot Harry would patronize. Floating on liquid courage, I seek out the grande dame, finding her ensconced in a corner booth with Yves St Laurent and Pierre Berger, and three of their impossibly beautiful models. I start to back away but Sylvie waves for me to sit with them. I know I'm pretty good looking, but being next to these models makes me feel like I'm from Planet Plain. The fashion designers are cordial but soon get up to dance. The models ask me about my music, and one says that if I were taller, I could walk the runway. Then they argue in French over this, and drift off to the dance floor. Sylvia laughs, spins her forefinger around at the side of her head. "Belle mais fou!" Beautiful but crazy.

"Sylvie, do you know Harry Lamb?"

She thinks for a second. "Mais oui! Arree l'agneau!" Laughs. "Il est plus un loup que de l'agneau!" She generously translates for me, "He is more wolf than lamb."

How true. And of course he's been here. "Have you seen him lately?"

She touches my hand. "You love him." When I don't reply, she caresses my cheek. "I understand. I have not seen Harry for a while but will ask a few people." She embraces me and I flee as soon as the models return.

34

The recording studio is small but fully equipped. Since I'm not signed to a record label yet, these will just be demos, but my music – basic lead sheets with lyrics and chords – has been distributed on the music stands. Over the next ten minutes, the musicians drift in; guitar player, drummer, bass. The recording engineer sets up and tests mikes. I'm going to put down a basic guitar track first and then we'll add the other instruments, and the vocal.

The producers, Maurice and Marcel, have translated some of my lyrics into French. I read through them but can't be sure if the translation is any good. They could be dumb as mud and I wouldn't know the difference. Anxiety rises from my belly to my throat and I'm not sure if I can sing. I want to run out the door.

At that moment, the one I think is Maurice – he's tall, wiry, with a Mediterranean complexion and long dark hair – comes over and translates the new French words in excellent English. They're not bad at all. He takes my hand and assures me it will all be "merveilleux!" Marcel – short, with close-cropped blond hair and glasses – is talking to the musicians as they tune up. The guitar player looks over at me and winks. Maybe it will all be okay. The engineer moves the microphone closer to my guitar. I want to apologize to these excellent musicians for my not-so-great playing but it's time to start, so I just count off and dive in.

When I hear the playback it sounds thin and clumsy, but once the lead guitar, bass, and drums are added, it all comes to life. We break as the engineer works with it for a while, balancing the various instruments, and it's time for me to sing the English lyric, and then the French. The choked-up feeling starts again. Breathe. Think about how I felt when I wrote the song. Sing it to someone important and of course only one person comes to mind, despite my efforts to push him out. Fuck it. I sing the song to Harry, as if he is across the room, and when it's done, I can see Maurice and Marcel through the glass of the soundproof booth, nodding approval. Before I record the French version, I go over pronunciation with Maurice. He insists that my French sounds good and a little accent is charming. Europeans love to hear Americans singing in their languages.

The other two songs also go well. Maybe I *can* do this.

35

Few people are on the street at this late hour in Les Halles. An occasional delivery truck rattles by on the old cobblestones to unload provisions, and the surviving restaurants and bars are open late. I pass L'Escargot Montorgueil, the grand old restaurant, with its enormous golden snail over the entrance, and remember the night Monsieur Frochot took me here – how impressed I was by the ornate, hundred-year-old décor, the garlic-smothered snails, and the oozingly rich onion soup. So much has happened since then. I'm on my way to meet Alistair.

Aromas from the few surviving markets and restaurants waft past; garlic, brine, meat, pungent earthy mushrooms, the sweetness of fresh baking bread, and chocolate. In the window of a boucherie, a dead rabbit is strung up, all soft paws and dull, sightless eyes.

After several blocks, I reach the edge of *le trou;* acres of trenches and dirt, a few construction vehicles forsaken in the abandoned crater, the future shopping center. An old woman huddles in the doorway of a shuttered store, her patchy layers of clothing almost camouflaged against the wall's peeling posters on wood and cracked stone. She mutters to herself in French and what sounds like German, and I wonder if she's been there since World War II and perhaps thinks it's still going on.

On rue Montorgueil, Saint-Eustache, a towering gothic and Renaissance church modeled on Notre Dame, stands guard over Les Halles, as it has since the 1600s. On impulse, I push through the thick wooden door and find a cavernous space mostly empty except for a few lost souls who've taken shelter from the damp night. I like churches, although Catholicism was considered heretical in my denomination. Those bloody, graphic crucifixions, when a plain cross would do just fine.

The vaulted interior of Saint-Eustache contains spires reaching upward and stained-glass depictions of joy and pain, of the everlasting search for meaning. A voice whispers but when I turn around, no one is there. Sound reverberates randomly in the arched, empty space, and I'm hearing someone praying at the altar. Should I light a candle? I think you're supposed to do that. But I don't know what the ritual is.

Okay, wish me luck, Catholic god. I exit the church and turn the corner toward my destination.

Here it is. Le Corbeau Noir, the name inscribed over the door in copper script, as if it has once been a much fancier place. What is "corbeau" again? The answer appears as a large stuffed black bird over the bar. Quoth the raven:

What a dump.

This is where the cultured Alastair Nelson likes to hang out?

I settle on a high barstool, keeping a close grip on my purse, and I catch the eye of the bartender, a rail-thin giant. There are half a dozen patrons at the bar – some look as if they've been painted in place – and a few more at the tables. A vintage Wurlitzer in the corner is playing.

"La neige tombe sur la mer....C'est la fin de l'affaire."

"Kir," I tell the bartender. There's a large taxidermized crow on a shelf, its umber glass eyes glaring at me.

Like a phantom, here's Alastair, coming out of the washroom, making a last-minute adjustment to his fly. I pretend to be busy with my drink, then glance up with a convincingly pleased expression.

"My dear!" he greets me. "I thought you might have forgotten." He looks like he wishes I had.

"But Mr. Nelson, how could anyone forget you?"

He preens at this cheap flattery. "I see you have your drink already!" Puts some money on the bar and leads me to a small table, carrying our drinks.

"I wasn't sure this was the right place."

"You mean," he says with a grin, "there's another joint like this somewhere in Paris?" The pub's décor includes animal-print wallpaper and faux-fur upholstery. He raises his glass and lightly clinks mine. "Cheers, my dear! À votre santé! And how are you enjoying this fair city?"

"It's beautiful. But I only just got back. I had a gig in Tehran."

"Yes, yes, of course!" He looks at the door, as if expecting someone. Glances at his watch.

"I'm not keeping you, am I?"

"I was supposed to meet a business associate. He's quite late." He tosses the whiskey down and signals the bartender for another round. "He was just dropping by for a moment. Nothing that would interfere with our rendezvous."

"Rendezvous? Is that what this is?"

"Well, no, I didn't mean—"

"Some wonderful painting to sell? Your business associate?"

"What? Yes, a painting."

I take in the dusty lights that flicker like strobes along the edges of the bar, a man whose face resembles old leather, and a woman with jaggedly cropped metallic red hair, laughing too loud.

"I used to go-go dance in places like this."

His eyes get wide. "I would like to have seen that. Did you wear what you wore in *Au Naturel!*"

"I don't want to disappoint you, but we weren't nude for the whole show."

"Oh, well, a little goes a long way." He's looking at me now as if my clothes are transparent. "And how did you get to be in that show?"

"It's funny, but I saw the show when it was in previews. A blind date took me. Guess he thought he'd get lucky because he spent so much on the tickets." At Alistair's raised eyebrow, I add, "He didn't. But I thought the actors were gorgeous, and having so much fun, so a few months later when there was a casting call for a replacement, I auditioned."

"And was it fun to do?"

"Absolutely!"

"You're making wish I weren't a married man."

I'm guessing that hasn't stopped him in the past. "Oh, Alistair…" I fake sigh. "Remember that gift you asked me to take to Christopher Fargate?"

"Of course, the Bahador figurine. Shame about Chris, wasn't it?"

"He seemed young to just drop dead."

"Life is full of surprises, isn't it? Of course, the sonofabitch sold my Bahador, didn't he?" He swigs his drink. "And then it went astray, I heard. The figurine, that is. Not Chris. Although I suppose you could say that death is the ultimate 'going astray.'"

"That was my fault – the thing 'going astray.'"

"Was it? But no major harm done, it was worth a bit but not priceless, and it will likely turn up again on the black market." He places his hand over mine and leaves it there, dry and bloodless. "You know, you really are an exquisite young woman. Some artist ought to paint you. I may know someone you could sit for, and then you'd be immortalized for posterity. Perhaps wearing your *Au Naturel!* costume." He finds this quite amusing.

I withdraw my hand. "I felt so bad about the figurine. I couldn't help but wonder where it came from originally."

"I picked it up after the war. My unit was stationed in Iran. Dear, don't worry about it."

"Did you ever hear that someone wrote a story about it? The Bahador figurine?"

"A story? I don't know but it picked up some legend along the way; a lightning rod for the 'resistance.'"

"Which resistance?"

"Every one of them! Wherever some rabble think they are being 'persecuted.'"

I excuse myself to find the ladies room. It's in the back, past a storage room, and a tiny kitchen that looks like cockroaches would be the specialty of the house. When I get back, feeling as if I could use a shower, Alistair has a few more drinks on the table.

"You must be awfully busy," I prompt him. "With your art sales."

"Always, always. But art is just a small corner of my life."

The jukebox plays loud and bright – *"it's a wild world.."*

Alistair stands, a bit unsteadily. "Excuse me, but I must make a call." He heads to the back of the bar.

I dump the contents of my drink into a planter.

There is his overcoat, limp as a Dali clock over the back of his chair. I slide a hand into one of the pockets; keys, cigarettes. I don't know what I'm looking for. The other pocket contains his kid leather gloves. Keys. One is a hotel key to the Ritz. And a business card. The person he was supposed to meet? I take a quick look. ***International Brokers, Global Assets Ltd.*** A UK phone number. I slip it back into the pocket. A few more minutes pass and I wonder if he's gone out a rear exit into the night.

But, no, here he comes. "Darling Rebecca! I'm so glad you came to keep me company this lonely night! You know," he lowers his voice, "the first time I saw you I thought you were a Jewess, and your name, from the Old Testament, well…"

"Would it matter?"

185

"Only if you wanted to have my children!"

"No chance of that." I laugh as if I were joking.

"I know, dear, I'm way too old." Another sip of his scotch. "I fought them in 1947, you know, when they were taking Palestine from us. Tenacious bastards, you have to give them credit. But they'll lose the next round, I can guarantee it," he says with a self-satisfied grin.

"Why do you say that?"

Alistair leans close and whispers, "Three million Jews. Thirty million Arabs." He sniffs. "It's all mathematics, isn't it? Human history. Who has the most wins, more people, more weapons, more blood to spill."

His pure coldness makes me shudder inside. "I never thought of it that way." I gaze at him with eyelash-blinking, feigned admiration.

Tapping his head with a forefinger, "You have to be smart," he preens. "Money buys power. Power buys people. People are dispensable. You see, my dear, what's important is to get the right people in power. Power and money, that's what makes the world go 'round. If I've learned anything in my life, it's that when people are down, they will do absolutely anything. Principles are wonderful if you aren't in need. And who among us isn't in need at one time or another? People are, basically, scum."

"I think there are good people. People who stand up for things they believe in."

"Of course! Of course! My personal 'cause', if you will, is to see that every miserable Jew is gone from Palestine, even if we have to blow the place to Kingdom Come. Which may happen soon. This isn't offensive to you, is it?"

I shake my head, keeping down the words I'd really like to say to him. And I'm realizing that my family – *my family* – was of the same mind. Although they looked at it as a kindness; as long as the Jews accept Jesus, they will be saved at the Rapture. Of course, if they don't convert, they'll be doomed to Hell with the rest of non-Christian mankind. Maybe the problem is religion itself.

I move closer to him. "Does any of this have to do with Iran? It's all so complicated, isn't it?" I sigh.

"Dear, this is just boring political talk."

"Oh, no, it's *fasc*inating. I so rarely get to talk to anyone so worldly and experienced." Good god, what a load of crap. "And you deal with so much wonderful art!"

"Yes, yes, I've always made money. I learned how at a young age. I started poor, you know. Spent the first half of my life working the angles of the art world. Got quite good at it. I'm worth a bit, you know."

"I'm sure you are."

"But I'd rather hear about you. Have you landed yourself a record contract yet?"

"I'm very close."

"I will play your record until it wears out!" He regards me, eyes narrowed. "As I recall, you were in touch with Harry Lamb?"

"Not lately." Hearing Harry's name kicks me in the gut.

"Too bad, I've been trying to contact him. We owe him some money. Some pictures he placed with us last year sold at auction."

"I saw him when I was in Iran. He mentioned you'd been working together on…a project. A big 'art' collection at a storage facility out in the middle of nowhere. A strange place."

"Really." His eyes narrow and all the starched jollity goes out of him. "You, uh, visited the storage facility?"

"It was just a fuel stop."

"I see."

The bar begins to empty, as if someone has pulled a plug. Alistair mutters, "You want to know the truth? I hate Paris. She's like the most beautiful woman in the world that you know you can't have, and she knows it, too, and just wants to stick it to you." His hand slips and he knocks over his glass. "My wife's going to have my head in a sling if I don't make this work. Is that a phrase?" he slurs. "Arm in a sling, not head. Head in a guillotine. Figures the French would invent that one."

"If what doesn't work?"

"Your friend Harry's big fucking deal." He puts his first two fingers to his lips. "Shhh. That's a secret. When it's done, we'll all retire to the south of France!" He pulls a soggy handkerchief from his jacket pocket and blows his nose. The first time I met Alistair, in New York with Harry last year, he seemed like the most elegant person in the world. Now strands of silver hair fall limp across his forehead. He clutches nervously at his tie, as if it might choke him. He's a living, soused, cadaver.

"Anyesha – my wife – is smarter than I am! She told me Harry was a bad bet." He coughs. "You don't need to worry about all this *merde* that's going on in the world, but just between you and me – I can trust you, right? Your boyfriend Harry—"

"He's not my boyfriend."

"—thought he could con the people who made him in the first place. Got Fargate to go along with him."

"What did Harry do?"

He tries to light another cigarette. I steady the lighter in his hand. "He was like a son to me! And how does he repay me? Betrayal! No one betrays Alistair Nelson." He pats my arm. "But don't worry, it all works out in the end. It always does."

"You know where to find him?"

He looks at me with a sly grin. "Why, Rebecca. Right here in this ragged little dive. Don't tell me you didn't know that?" He looks around. "But it looks like the wretched piece of shit stood us both up."

The jukebox goes silent. I think my heart has stopped, too. We're the last people in Le Corbeau Noir. The stuffed raven and the bartender both glower at us. "Fermé!" the bartender calls out, stacking chairs on tables, as if we might not have gotten the point that he's closing.

Alistair lurches to his feet. "Well, my dear, I suppose I should get you into a taxi."

"I think I should get *you* into a taxi." I put on my coat with some awkward help from Alistair. Outside, the bartender rolls down the shutters, closes the gate, and takes off on his moped in a puff of exhaust. No one else is on the street. The buzz of the moped fades into the night.

The massive construction site of le *trou* is the Grand Canyon behind a makeshift fence. A rat skitters along the gutter and disappears down a sewer grating. The slightest sound reverberates against the cracking walls and dirty windows of the abandoned markets.

"Taxi, taxi, where is a taxi?" Alistair mutters, looking up and down the street. "Come, let's go over to Montmartre, there's bound to be some poor bloke out looking for a fare." He takes my hand and starts to lead me into the street, but trips on an untied shoelace on his black oxfords. "Oh, for fuck's sake." He kneels down to tie it, his back to the street, his foot on the curb.

We've stopped but I still hear footsteps. A shadow moves. There's the quick blaze of a flaring match in a doorway. I get a fleeting glimpse of his face.

Mon amour.

36

*H*e's wearing the gray raincoat and a brimmed hat, like someone out of an old movie. Seeing my expression, he quips, "I told you I'd be back." His attention turns from me to Alistair. "Hello, Nelson. Sorry I'm late. Had trouble finding a cab. But I'm sure Rebecca kept you entertained." He gives me that heart-breaking smile.

Shoelace tied, Alistair clambers to his feet. "To be sure, but I've had a few too many and it's probably not a good time to discuss business. Must get the lady home."

"Don't worry, I'll see the lady gets home safely."

"The 'lady,'" I reply to both of them, "can damn well take care of her fucking self."

Harry says to me, "You don't need to be here. Let's meet," he checks his watch, "in an hour. At Harry's Bar. It's not far from here."

"I know where it is but the Metro's closed, you know, so—"

"We'll find a cab."

"Thanks but I think I'll stay."

He gives up. "Fine."

Meanwhile, Alistair has gained at least an imitation of sobriety.

Adrenalin will do that. "Harry, we can certainly work things out. Let's find a drink. How about Sylvie's? They're open all night."

Of course Alistair has been there, too. It's as if my life has come full circle.

"I think I'll take my payoff now," Harry says.

"You don't seriously think I'm carrying around half a million quid?"

Having gone through Alistair's coat pockets, I'm inclined to believe him.

Harry is as calm as if they're discussing the weather. "Then I guess your hotel is our next stop. The Ritz, right?"

"Not this time," he lies. "Too ostentatious."

"Actually…" I nod at the pocket of Alistair's coat. "You do have a room key."

He flushes pink. "You went through my coat, you cunt?"

"Looks that way."

"The Ritz, then." Harry takes a step closer to Alistair. "Let's go."

Alistair reaches into his jacket's inner pocket. "Not tonight." There's a click. Harry sees the knife at the same time I do, and moves quickly. Alistair sidesteps, thrusts out, ripping the fabric of Harry's coat sleeve.

Blood trickles down below his cuff. "You sonofabitch." Harry spins Alistair around, pulls him off the curb into the street and punches him in the face. Alistair reels back and kicks out, a judo kick, catching Harry in the stomach. Harry drops. Rage propels me forward, straight at Alistair. I want to rip his face off, but the knife is still in his hand, and he stabs out with it, inches away so I just slam into him as hard as I can, and then I'm on the ground, dizzy from the impact. When I look up, Harry is standing, with a stunned look, and Alistair has vanished. I follow Harry's gaze to *le trou*.

That's when I see a hand, encased in its beige kid glove, reaching over the top of the construction site. The fence is smashed where he went through, and he's trying desperately to find a secure hold, to pull himself back up. Harry steps forward. I take a cautious step to the edge of the vast construction hole. Alistair is clutching a scaffolding board. He looks up at me but I don't move. The board splits and collapses. Harry and I are forced back as the sides of the ditch begin to give way; an avalanche of dirt, old rocks, concrete, iron, all tumbling down, down into the hole in the middle of the city, taking the body of Alistair Nelson far, far astray.

37

I can hear my heart beating in double time. The expression "heart in your throat" has real meaning. A car turns down the street. Harry pulls me back into the shadows. The car passes by. He digs into his pocket for a cigarette, lights it, inhales deeply. I can just make out his face, and it has a half smile. The ooh-ahh ooh-ahh of a police car or ambulance pierces the night. We both freeze. It Dopplers in another direction.

Blood drips from Harry's cut arm. We remove his coat and jacket, and push up the shirt sleeve. I take off his tie and wrap it around the wound. "Does it hurt?"

"Of course it fucking hurts."

Then we're kissing. I taste the fresh smoke and the specific Harry-flavor I love, and the night falls away for a moment. He has me against the wall in the doorway, lifts up my skirt, pushes aside my panties and we're fucking standing up and I can't pull him in fast enough, deep enough, it's over in a minute. He doesn't pull out right away. It occurs to me that I could get pregnant, and I just don't care. Let it happen. Or not. After another minute, we break apart, and begin to laugh, giddy as children.

A cracking sound snaps us back into reality, but it's just another avalanche in *le trou*. This reminds me that someone has just died there and I guess I should feel bad – or at least feel something besides primitive desire.

"But what if he isn't dead?" I whisper. My leg is bruised where I fell, and my long coat has streaks of dirt. I try to brush it off.

"He's got ten tons of Les Halles on top of him."

"We should call…" I don't finish the sentence.

Harry grabs my hand and we're walking away from *le trou* – then we're running.

38

*H*arry's been staying in a flat near the Louvre, off *rue Saint-Honoré*. We take the rattling cage elevator up to the fourth-floor apartment, which has fancy furniture that looks like it's been there since the French Revolution. Framed, yellowing reproductions on the walls. Deep-blue velvet curtains. The windows are practically glued shut, and dirty.

"Whose place is this?"

"Like it?"

"In a past-life sort of way." In the bedroom, I push my hand on the mattress. It creaks with softness.

"Just a bloke I know. Rich fucker. Spends most of his time in the Riviera."

I pace the place, checking the windows, the door, the bathroom, not for anything in particular but just out of a general sense of unease. What about Clementine Solis and everything she told me? When the news comes of Alistair's disappearance, will I be arrested? She has no idea I actually saw Alistair. Harry's in the bedroom. He flops on the bed, smiles and beckons me over. It's not even sexual; his gaze is filled with affection.

I sit a few feet away, on the edge of a gilded chaise longue. "Someone told me some... things about you. Bad things. I want to know if they're true."

"Someone? Alistair?"

"No, not Alistair. In fact, it was this...other person who sent me to meet Alistair."

He turns to face me, leaning on his arm. "Who?"

"I'd rather not say."

A half-smile. "Very mysterious."

I focus on the bedroom's thick drapes with their old-fashioned floral pattern. "This person said you were involved in things like, well, weapons trafficking. To criminals and dictators. Countries that support terrorism."

Harry stares at me, then bursts out laughing. "Rebecca, are you serious? Who told you this?"

"There are pictures."

"Of me?"

"No, but—"

"You believed this bullshit?"

"No, yes, I don't know what to believe! She had papers, and your name was on them, and these photos of bodies."

"She?" He's on his feet, face red with anger. I have a flash of fear that he'll turn it on me. He raises his fist, brings it down hard on the back of the chaise. "God, you believed all this!"

"I don't know, I don't know! That place in the desert, there were crates of guns!"

"That had nothing to do with me!"

"I'm not an idiot, Harry. Or maybe I am."

"No. You're not." He sits back down on the edge of the bed and rubs his temples with his fingertips. "I've got the most blasted headache. Do you have an aspirin?"

I find one in my purse. He swallows it dry.

"All your secrets, the coming and going, what am I supposed to think?"

"That I'm an arsehole of a boyfriend?" He presses his fingers on his forehead.

"Well, that goes without saying."

"I thought I explained it all, back in Tehran."

"You said a lot of stuff. But that's before I saw all the—"

"Evidence?" He sighs. "Rebecca, I'm beat. Can't we get some sleep and talk about this in the morning?" He moves to one side, leaving an empty space for me. "Please."

I stay put. "Who are you? You're like sand, constantly shifting with the tides, and every time I try to pin you down, you shapeshift again. You're as fickle as the wind."

"You're a poet. Although that 'fickle as the wind' is a bit of a cliché."

I'm exhausted too, but I can't let this go. "Just tell me the truth. If you're the monster of the photos, I want to know. I want to know who I'm fucking, who I said, 'I love you' to, and if that makes me a monster, too, then so be it. At least I'll know what we are."

He sits up and lights a cigarette. The smoke curls around his head like a halo, which is the height of contradiction. He doesn't look at me.

"This 'monster' was born in Lambeth. In the 1930s, it was a shithole of working class – and out-of-working class during the Depression – factory town. So, meet Harry Hoggard, son of a butcher. Mother was a slag, who ran off before I was three. There were a few brothers and a sister, from different men, and they were scattered." Harry's lapsed into an accent that sounds a lot like Cockney. "I was five or six when the war broke out, and our little South London town was hit hard when the bombing started. Daddy had the misfortune to be under a building that got bombed to smithereens by the Jerrys – the krauts – and I moved in with the 'charming' Aunt Kit and Uncle Fred. A right old bastard Freddy was, getting drunk at the pubs and then home to beat up whoever happened to be there, Kit, or me, or one of their kids. Six people in two rooms in a flat three floors up, overlooking an alley where the classy tenants tossed their garbage." He stops, turns around to face me. "Had enough?"

I'm not even sure he isn't making this up, or borrowing the plot of an old movie. But his face shows the pain of recollection. "No. Go on."

He crushes the cigarette in an ashtray and lights another. "This all sounds like a Dickens novel, doesn't it?" Without waiting for an answer, he continues, "I stuck it out with dear old Kit and Fred until I was old enough – and big enough – to knock Uncle Freddy to the floor. With a few kicks for good measure. One of the most satisfying moments of my life. I was strong from working in Freddy's little hauling business – hauling paving stones or bricks or wood or whatever – and now I'm on the street, fifteen years old with nothing in my pockets but lint and nothing but my callow good looks—" here he glances at me with a grin "—and a talent for... persuasion." Harry sighs, shakes his head as if jogging loose more memories. "The war is two years gone and London still looks like a pile of rubble but capitalism is stirring. The soldiers that survived are home and everyone is putting the pieces together. I changed my last name from Hoggard to Lamb – for Lambeth, y'see. A farewell to my hometown. I worked odd jobs, ran errands for bookies, drugs for dealers, girls for rich men. Yes, don't look at me that way, I did it all. Mea culpa. Mea maxima culpa." He doesn't sound all that sorry.

Harry gets up, stretches, and yawns, then takes off his shirt and undershirt. I can't help but notice the lean muscles, the skin like firm silk. I change the subject in my mind, away from his body and back to his words. He's wide awake now, checking the window as if someone might be watching from the street.

"And so began the evolution of Harry Hoggard, slum rat, to Harrold Doyle Lamb, gentleman." He emphasizes the upper-class accent. "I listened to the BBC a lot, how they spoke. It's what they call 'Received Pronunciation – RP. If you've ever seen *My Fair Lady* you know what I mean." He laughs. "It didn't hurt that I had a posh lady friend, capital

L, who helped smooth things out. Because the first thing the toffs judge you on is how you talk." He lapses back into South London. "Wha' a lah'a bovver!"

"What?"

Crisply, "What a lot of bother."

"Where did the 'Doyle' come from?'

He laughs. "Arthur Conan Doyle, author of *Sherlock Holmes*. I figured if I was going to be the creator of a fictional character…" He pads into the small kitchen and opens the fridge, commenting, "Wasteland." Finds a beer and cracks it open. "Want one?"

"God, no." What I want is two days' sleep. I've lost track of time. There's a clock radio by the bed that says six, but I'm not sure if that's morning or night.

I slide back the drapes to a mauve dawn. Lights flickering on all over the city.

Harry leaves his beer on the night table. It has a marble top that would certainly stain, so I move the can to the floor. Then I think about tripping and the beer spilling all over the antique carpet, so I get up and return it to the kitchen. Wondering whose flat this is, I check out the bathroom and open the cabinet. Makeup. A razor. A box of Tampax? Men's shaving cream. A unisex deodorant. I could just ask him but that's so much like an interrogating female. Which is exactly what I am. I shut the door, pee, and then return to the bedroom.

"The art business? How on earth did you get into that?"

"Ah, my grand career. Lady Charlotte – that was her name – asked me to sell a picture for her. Stuffy portrait of some old, titled ancestor that stared down at her in the London townhouse and she hated it. 'Get a good price,' she told me. I'd met a few buyers and sellers in my other 'businesses' so I made a few calls and offloaded the thing to a collector of upper-class toff portraits. Probably passing it off as his pedigree. There's a collector for everything. Took my commission and a career was born. The talent of persuasion came in handy. And, it turned out, I had an eye for art. I took a few courses in art history, learned all about the Renaissance, the Dutch masters, Romanticism, Rococo, Impressionists – stopped there because I'm not much fond of the moderns. But it's more about reading people, figuring out what they want to live with – paintings, that is. Match the perfect Pissarro to the patron of the arts who knows nothing about art, only what he likes. And is proud of his ignorance."

I watch Harry as he talks, noticing the way he twitches the cigarette back and forth, the way the tendons of his wrists contract, all these details that make up the complete man. It's as if I keep meeting him anew, layer by layer, and each more intriguing than the last. A wave of tenderness comes over me, for his past (assuming it's true), imagining him as that little boy in Lambeth. This is different than the euphoric passion, the wild nights we've shared. This is someone I could love for my life. He looks at me and our thoughts seem to meld in synchrony. It's a scary feeling, like being on the edge of a cliff and looking down, knowing that if you took one more step… All this time, I guess I never thought of him beyond the moment. It's as if we've stepped off the cliff together, holding hands and believing, with no evidence to support it, that the parachute will open and we'll float safely to the ground.

As long as we keep hiding here, we're safe, because out there in the world are the devils. Or we're the devils.

Fatigue comes over me like a lead blanket. I lie down, facing the window, keeping a distance between us. He moves over, puts his arm around me, and we remain like that, the only sound an occasional car speeding by in the street below.

39

I don't even remember falling asleep, but I'm on the bed, still dressed, and Harry is lying next to me, also dressed, and snoring lightly.

The night begins to come back to me, in glimpses. Alistair in the bar. Harry's arrival. The fight. The "accident." Running. This apartment. My life has become a series of bad decisions. I once had a moral compass, but it appears I dropped it somewhere over the Atlantic Ocean. Or was it the English Channel? Tehran? Does it matter? And Harry's Dickensian tale of deprivation turned to ambition and crime is a movie playing in my head.

I've lost myself, the way I always have when I fall in love. But nothing like this. I want my self back. I want my religion back, but you can't resurrect something that was made out of air and fairytales. Answers and explanations where there are none. Afraid of death? There's Heaven. Hoping some terrible person will get his or her comeuppance? Hey, there's Hell! Something good happens? It's a miracle! Something bad happens? It's God's will! But I want to believe again. I want the comfort, the crutch, the delusion.

I inch off the bed, trying not to wake him. Am I done with him? I don't know. I only know that I have to get out. But I don't want to desert him, to disappear the way he's done. I don't want him to worry, so I grab a piece of paper from my notebook, and write, "Sylvie's tomorrow midnight, love you." I fold the note and place it by his wallet. I also take some of the cash he's left on the dresser.

It's an ordinary morning in Paris. No one pays any attention to the girl in the scuffed coat, wearing heels, looking like she's barely slept. I walk in the general direction of the 7th Arrondissement, on the other side the Seine. This is the warm, flowery, Paris spring day I've heard so much about.

I cross the Seine on Pont des Arts, one of the many Paris pedestrian bridges. The Louvre is behind me now. I immediately regret leaving the note, and consider going back for it. But I don't have a key and the last thing I want to do is face him right now. At least he doesn't know anything about Max's flat. Right now I wish I had never set eyes on Harry Lamb. Or Harry Hoggard. At the same time, I want him inside me, enveloping me. I would die for him. I could kill him.

I'm near the other side, heading towards Saint Germain des Pres, and Max's apartment. The past twenty-four hours seem to land on me and it's hard to take a breath. I pause at the embankment and look at the river, the gray water.

It all comes back to me. Not last night but years ago. When they all died in the river. My family – Mama, Papa, my Aunt Bess and Uncle Bill, and cousins Joe and Carol. I'm in the van with them, the snow is coming down, the road so icy. Why didn't you stop and pull over, Papa? So stubborn; he'd make it home, he always did, staring ahead, gaze unwavering, trusting in God to protect them, but then the tires slip sideways, he rights the car, the road turns to glass, the edge of the road so close, too close, there's the ravine, he spins the wheel, it doesn't work, they're gliding, flying, screaming, praying. It's simply impossible that this is happening. No one woke up that morning thinking, *This is the last day of my life*. The wind and snow slam the van as it takes to the air, then it rolls and rolls, into the icy river. The van fills with water. Gone.

Gone.

I sink to my knees, bent over.

A woman stops and says something, probably asking if I'm okay. I manage to nod. She helps me up and walks with me to the end of the bridge and over to a statue, where I sit on its broad base. I assure the woman I'm fine. She looks concerned but leaves.

I have no family. The thought is almost a surprise, although it's been a fact for these eight years. An orphan. Why wasn't I with them? Why them and not me?

A few feet away, a musician is playing a small accordion. I don't know the tune but it's surely a love song. Lyrics run through my head and I'm reaching for the pencil in my bag and my little notebook, to write the words down before they get lost. It's hard to see through the tears. The musician has already moved on to another melody and I've filled a page with a song. Maybe surviving is all that matters. I can't bring them back. I can only move forward. My own life. Whatever that is.

40

I start to put the key in the door of Max's apartment and realize it's already open. The music playing – Elton John's "Have Mercy on the Criminal" – should have tipped me off. Inside, it's booming loud, and Max doesn't hear me come in. He's in the bedroom, unpacking. I yell his name and he turns around, a startled look turning into a grin and open arms. Then he takes a better look at my scraped arm, scuffed shoes, and dirty dress, and frowns. He turns down the music on the stereo.

"What the hell?"

"Don't ask." I slump onto the bed and kick off my shoes.

"Were you mugged?"

"No."

"Fall down a well?"

"I really don't want to talk about it. I could use some coffee."

He goes to the kitchen and puts water on to boil for the French press. I make my way to the bathroom and run the shower. It's like washing off the night. If only I could rinse off reality. Harry has no idea where I'm staying. Clementine doesn't know either. I feel like I've gone into witness protection, if only for now. I put on Max's terrycloth robe and emerge to the scent of fresh coffee.

He's making an omelet and has put out two plates.

"So how was Spain?"

"Very Spanish."

I open the windows in the living room, thinking about the heavy drapes in Harry's friend's flat. The city sounds are intrusive and comfortingly familiar. Is Harry waking up now? Realizing I'm gone?

We sit down to eat like an old married couple, but Max seems distracted. He leafs through the *International Herald Tribune*; I open a book that's lying on the table, *Watership Down*, and read the first few pages. "Rabbits! They're so cute. But why does it open with quotes from a Greek play?" Not that I've ever finished reading a Greek play.

"Portending tragedy."

I close the book.

"Rebecca, I know this will sound…well, a friend of mine is going to visit and stay here, and it could get a bit crowded. I mean, there's no hurry and I can help you find a place."

"Your Spanish friend?"

He nods. "She's English and doing her post doc in French lit…"

I tune out, already thinking about where I'll go, and pissed off that he's got a girlfriend when I have no right to be proprietary. "English." "Post doc." Well, la de da. I'm up and gathering my things. Not even finishing the meal. I just want to get out. Is this a sign that I should go back to Harry? I'm not even sure of his address but can probably find it. No, bad idea.

"I didn't mean you have to go this minute."

"No problem, I was going to tell you—"

"She won't be here for a couple of days—"

"—that I found another place in, uh, over near the Louvre and it's great, a one-bedroom with big windows and a huge bathtub and I can move in today!"

He sits down, unconvinced. In ten minutes I've stuffed the suitcase, and gathered up the detritus I've left around in my stay here. I grab the guitar. If I've forgotten anything, I can pick it up later. Wow, have I ever gotten good at packing and clearing out fast! If there were an award for this. Leaving is what I do best. Harry and I share that gift.

"I'll call and give you the new address. Thanks for breakfast!" Out the door, letting it slam shut.

Now I have to find someplace to go. Definitely not back to Harry. The cash I took from him is more than I expected and in French currency, so that's good. Certainly enough for a couple of nights at a nice hotel. Not the Hotel Paradis with its stuffy, closet-sized rooms. I remember a very pretty place I passed when I visited Chris Fargate's gallery near the Bois du Boulogne, and thinking then that I wished I could afford it. Probably full but worth a try. I even remember the name: Les Bois: The Woods.

In a tabac, I find the number in their tattered phone book. The hotel has an available room.

An hour later, ensconced in the relative luxury of Les Bois, with fresh, room service coffee, croissants, and a telephone with free local calls, I can finally relax. First call is to my agent or manager or whatever he is. The answering service picks up – Frochot is probably out to lunch, dining with a client – so I leave the hotel and room numbers. Max? He can wait a bit. Clementine? This douses the good mood like a bucket of ice water. I could call her and make up some crap about my evening with Alistair; he never showed up or he left early, and said nothing of any interest. Fuck it.

Getting outside feels like a good idea. Out of curiosity I walk past the former Christopher Fargate Gallery. Unsurprisingly, it's closed, although the name is still there on the discreet brass placard. There's mail sticking out under the door. The curtains inside are closed. I wonder if Chris died in his gallery or at home. If he had any family. I really knew nothing about him and have a sting of regret that I never thanked him for connecting me to my agent.

Around the corner is a café. I miss the get-togethers with Max, Ellen, and Jimmy. I don't really have friends. Just acquaintances. What with moving around, and then, in New York, where you'd get close to the cast of a show until it ended and everyone dispersed. Boyfriends came and went. A girl pal for a while, then she'd hook up with a guy and be gone. I envy the groups of young women shopping together, laughing, going to the movies, to clubs, sharing their lives. The mothers and daughters who are best friends. You're a loner, people have told me. But is that a choice or a sentence?

Back at the hotel, the room phone is ringing. Frochot. My demos went to the A&R man at a small but prestigious European record label. They want to meet with me tomorrow at eleven at the record producers' office. I write down the address, and make Frochot repeat it. He's very happy. I'm very terrified.

41

The two producers who did my demos, Maurice and Marcel, work out of a tidy brownstone on a hushed street that is walking distance from the hotel. It's as if all this were ordained. No, not by God. Unless there's a special music god like the Greeks and Romans had, among their assortment of gods. I always liked that idea; you could pick and choose. Apollo was the god of music and he played the lyre. Liar. Harry. I push the thought away.

The office is homey, with built-in bookshelves filled with record albums and tapes. Framed awards on the walls. A dark-brown leather sofa faces the wide windows looking out at the park. If I ever doubted that these guys were top drawer, my doubts have been dispelled. Maurice, the tall, better looking one, pulls out a chair for me. Marcel, the shorter, more talkative one, has my demos and my new contract with EMI Records, the famous European label.

The doorbell rings. It's Frochot, come to oversee the signing of the contract and to ensure his commission. There is much rapid chatter in French and apologetic looks at me, and the translations. A secretary brings in coffee and madeleines, as well as a bottle of Châteauneuf du Pape, and we toast each other with the blood-red wine in graceful goblets. I have a sense of unreality, as if I could wake up at any moment and find myself back in New York, in my tiny, roachy walk-up, trying to write a song that I'm certain no one will ever want to record.

Having a dream come true is confusing. You immediately assume you don't deserve it, or something terrible will happen to balance out the universe, or it will all vanish in a puff of smoke, like the Wicked Witch. But no purple smoke appears and I drink the wine, feeling the sun that streams in the window and the camaraderie of people with a common goal; to make music. *My* music. And money.

The real recording will begin in a few days. The demo tracks are usable, but there's much to be done to make this a commercial record. They set up a photo session and an appointment with the publicist. Then it's time to leave this fairytale world for a while. There's a lot of double air-kissing and congratulating and promises that I will be a star.

This star returns to the hotel to collapse.

42

For Sylvie's, I've put on shimmering silver, wide-leg pants and a black halter top cut low at the sides. No bra. No underwear at all. The silky material caresses my bare thighs. Strap-on platform heels give me another three inches of height, to nearly six feet. I love the ripple of attention from males and females alike as I undulate through the thickening crowd, not sure if I'll see Harry here or ever see him again. Sylvie is at her usual spot with her entourage, and she beckons me to squeeze into the banquette. When there's a brief lull in the French chatter, I lean towards her and say, "I signed a record contract." She immediately orders champagne and we toast. The other people, whom I've never seen before, join in the toast and congratulations. I'm looking around for Harry because he's the only one I really want to share the news with. As the moments tick well past midnight, a hollow ache takes over inside my chest.

Sylvie sees him first. "Arree!" she calls out to the handsome man in the three-piece charcoal-gray suit. I'm reminded of the first time we met and how struck I was by his elegance. I'm not sure I can put this together with the Harry Hoggard he so vividly depicted, and it amuses me to know his secret. I'm tempted to greet him with, *Mr.*

Hoggard, I believe we've met but restrain myself. He kisses my hand. Sylvie, who, of course, knows all about us, grins and hands him a glass to celebrate my news.

"What took you so long?" I remark.

Harry doesn't take his eyes off me, even as he downs the champagne, and it occurs to me that we are destined to meet over and over again, like being born repeatedly, with all the pain and joy that entails.

We're on the dance floor, bouncing about to French and American hits. Then it's the Roberta Flack rendition of *The First Time Ever I Saw Your Face* drawing me into Harry's arms.

A few hours later, as we leave the club, there are, as usual, a line of black limos waiting for the rich and famous to emerge. The driver door opens on one, and the chauffeur steps out, along with a heavyset man wearing a brown leather jacket. They look at us.

"Really, Harry, you didn't have to!" Although I love a limo ride.

He frowns. "I didn't."

The two men flank us, and it happens quickly. The rear door opens, and we're propelled inside. There's another man in the limo, sitting at the far side of the dimly lit interior, a hat drawn low on his face, revealing only a short beard. The chauffeur takes his place behind the wheel while leather jacket pushes us into the seats facing the fedora guy. He then takes his seat, revealing a gun at his hip. I'm thinking this must be a joke, but Harry's expression suggests otherwise. He reaches for the door but it's locked. The car is moving, the dark-tinted windows closed. The chauffeur's divider slides up. It's just Harry and me and the two strange men.

"What the fuck is this?" Harry says.

No answer. I can't tell where we're headed. Harry squeezes my hand. I look at the fedora man. There's something vaguely familiar about him and I realize it's the scarf around his neck. I've seen it somewhere before. The fat guy's gun is black and stubby. Probably a 9mm. We shot that in Missouri at a target range. Papa and Gabriel and me. It's the same kind of gun Gabriel used to kill the doctor.

After several minutes of driving in silence, the fedora guy pushes his hat back and says, "Nice to see you, Harry. Becky."

Christopher Fargate.

Harry shows no reaction, except for a small movement of his jaw. "Fargate." His voice is as level as his demeanor. "You're looking well. For a dead man."

Chris gives a short laugh. The fat one grins, caressing his gun.

"Whatever this is about," Harry says, "I'm sure we can work it out."

"I'm sure we can." Chris lights a cigarette.

We drive on, up into a hilly area – Montmartre? Pigalle? – and dark, narrow streets, at last turning into an alley and then a garage under a building. There is no one around. We're hustled out of the limo.

When Christopher Fargate gets out of the car, I can see that he's thinner than when I last saw him, several months ago. His hair is cut short, with more gray. There are streaks of gray in his beard. He looks ten years older.

The chauffeur pulls down the garage door behind us. We're in some kind of storage warehouse. Crates are piled high against one wall. There's a desk and a few chairs. A weak overhead light. Peeling walls showing the stains of old water seepage.

Lovely.

The fat goon searches us, while the chauffeur leans in a doorway, lighting a cigarette. Chris sits and gestures for us to do the same. The fat goon, cigarette dangling from his lips, pulls Harry's hands behind the back of the chair and loops a rope around his wrists. They leave me unbound, I guess a female is too weak to matter.

Chris gets right to the point, staring at Harry. "The souvenir. I want it."

"Does it look like I have it on me?"

"Where is it?"

"I haven't a clue."

Chris turns to me. "Becky, am I supposed to believe a word he says?"

"You tell me."

We both contemplate the veracity of anything Harry Lamb says.

My mouth has gone dry. "I haven't seen the thing since Tehran. It went to your contact and that was the end of it."

Chris' chair creaks as he leans back. "Seems that it didn't." He sighs. "Look, I don't want to sound like a bloke in an old crime movie, but we can do this the easy way, or we can do it the hard way. Whichever, I'll end up finding out what I want to know." He rubs a hand across his forehead. "I'm squeamish. I don't like to see anything suffer. But these walls are thick, and we have lots of time. So, please…"

I glance at Harry, the pit in my stomach growing deeper. I'm incredibly thirsty and strangely detached, as if all this is happening in some alternate universe.

The fat goon approaches Harry and strikes him hard, across the face. His head snaps back and forward again. I jump up, lunging at the goon, only to be shoved back in the chair. This time they tie my hands, too.

"People, people," Fargate says, as if refereeing a game of softball that's gotten out of hand. "Is this necessary?"

Harry speaks up. His lip is bleeding. "No. It is not. The whole thing is ridiculous. Let me make a few calls and I'll track the…the souvenir down for you. And let Rebecca go. She has nothing to do with this."

"Really?" Chris' eyes narrow to slits. "Seems to me the last time I saw it, it was in her hands."

"I did what you said! I smuggled the fucking thing to Iran and gave it to the guy!" I'm lying, of course. The thing went to Harry. I have no idea what he did with it.

"Not according to the Iran contact." He speaks slowly, as if to a child. "And I tend to believe someone who's been tortured over someone protecting her boyfriend."

Hopelessness steals over me. Exhaustion. Please just let me wake up from this. "You trusted me to deliver it. I did that. Whatever happened after had nothing to do with me. Or Harry."

Harry offers, "I suggest you ask your friend Alistair Nelson about it."
That might be quite difficult.

"Last I heard," Harry continues, "Alistair was making a deal with
some Iranians. That's where your statue went, I'm guessing." Harry
adjusts in his chair. There's a reddening bruise on his face. "Alistair had
a flat in Paris – still has it I'm thinking – does a lot of business out of it,
keeps paintings stored. But you probably know that. You're barking up
the wrong tree here. I'll set things up with Alistair and I guarantee I can
get you the dough. And the paintings. Some good ones there."

Chris gets up and for a moment I think he's going to strike Harry
himself. But he walks from one side of the room to the other and back.

"Good ones?" Chris nods to his goon. "Nico, some water." Nico goes
through a door. We hear water running from a tap. He comes back a
moment later with a plastic carafe and some paper cups. Chris pours
himself a cup and downs it.

Harry stares at him. "By the way, how did you manage to rise from
the dead?"

I wonder if my life is going to end here, in a dilapidated garage
in a crummy Paris neighborhood, and if anyone will ever know what
happened to me. I also wonder why Chris Fargate, who has apparently been in hiding and pretending to be dead for several months, has
decided to reveal himself to us, unless he doesn't expect us to be alive
after tonight.

"I want the art and the figurine, and we'll split the money sixty/
forty," he says to Harry. "We both have an interest in a big payoff."

"Long as I get the sixty."

Chris laughs. We could be having a convivial night if you leave out
the abduction, the gun, and the seedy neighborhood.

"It's been a revelation to be 'dead.' It's like being invisible. You find
out who your friends are. And aren't. If there'd been a funeral, I could
have shown up. But there was no funeral because there was no body. I'd
already made arrangements with a funeral director I knew, who'd keep

his mouth shut. Christopher Fargate joined the ranks of the deceased, and I could get on with my life. First thing was tracking down the shit who screwed me on the pictures. That's you, Harry. And Alistair. But I'll settle with him next."

Harry and I glance sideways at each other.

"What do you want, Chris? Or whatever your name is now." Harry stretches his shoulders back. "Could you get this crap off our hands? It's not like we're armed. You want to talk business, we'll talk like civilized people."

Chris nods at Nico. He reluctantly releases our hands. I rub my wrists and bend them back and forth.

I glare at Chris. "How about a glass of that delicious-looking water."

"I'm not a bad guy, you know," he replies, pouring the water and handing it to me.

I gulp it down. "You just grabbed us at gunpoint."

There are a number of sealed boxes piled up, different shapes, some like the large, flat containers used to ship paintings. Probably stuff from his closed gallery. He could have been planning this whole death fake when I first met him.

Harry stands. Nico touches his gun. "Oh, relax," Harry tells him. "I'm just stretching my legs." To Chris, he says, "Got a piece of paper? I'll give you the address where you can find the art. Send your guy over there, get the stuff, bring it back. But let Rebecca go. She isn't involved in any of this and I'm sure she has no interest in announcing to the world that Christopher Fargate is still alive."

"Not in the least."

"I have a better idea," Chris says. "Nico and I will stay here with Becky, while Louie here," he nods at the chauffeur, "accompanies you to…" He looks at the address Harry wrote down. "22 rue Fleur."

That's where we just stayed. I'm fairly sure nothing is stashed there. I'm also pretty sure it isn't Alistair's flat. I can't imagine what Harry has up his sleeve.

"No," Harry replies. "Do you think I'm going to leave Rebecca alone here with…that." He gestures at Nico, who has limited English skills.

"You're in no place to negotiate, Lamb." Chris sits back, a cat with a canary in its sight. "But I'll stay here with Becky. Best to have two with you in case you try to pull anything."

Harry looks at me. I give a slight nod that it's okay. I'm not afraid of Christopher Fargate. Maybe I should be.

A moment later, Harry, Louie, and Nico leave in the limo.

43

Chris takes a pistol out of the desk drawer, and sits on the edge of the desk. The walls are thick, just as he said. The world has narrowed down to me and this man. I wonder what Harry is planning to do with those two guys and that apartment empty of the treasure they're after. I wonder what I'm going to do. I get up and move to the water pitcher, pouring another cupful. Chris stirs and tightens his grip on the gun.

I notice a radio on the desk, an old plastic one with an antenna. "How about some music?"

He raises an eyebrow. "Why, you want to dance?"

"Just a thought."

He switches it on and flips around the stations till he comes to one playing French pop music. Turns the volume low but still audible. Some bouncy song. Soon it will be one of mine. I hope it won't be posthumous.

I lean forward in the chair. "Remember that night when we were at Harry's bar, when I thought I saw Jean-Paul Belmondo, and it *was* Jean-Paul Belmondo? It was my second night in Paris and I thought it was the most glamorous thing ever. Me, a hick from the Midwest, in Europe with all those sophisticated people! People like you; Christopher

Fargate, big-time gallery owner. I was so impressed." I smile, and lower my gaze, looking up at him through my lashes.

"Ha!" But he looks flattered. "I was a bit drunk as I recall."

"Really? You seem like a guy who can hold his liquor." I stretch my arms up and back. "You were nice. You gave me that agent's name, and it turned out well. He got me a recording contract."

Chris' eyebrows go up.

"I'm hoping I'll still be alive to finish the record." I take a step toward him.

He flinches and lifts the gun. "I'm not fucking around here."

"No shit." I sit again and this time put my hands over my face. "I just…I'm just so tired."

Chris doesn't say anything.

"Do you have a sweater or a blanket or something? I'm freezing."

"You're not wearing much."

"I guess I forgot to wear my getting kidnapped outfit."

He grabs his coat and tosses it to me. It's a good wool tweed that reeks of tobacco.

"You must have gotten used to being a bit chilly, nude on stage and all." He has that knowing, prurient expression most men get when talking about *Au Naturel!* "Wish I'd seen the show. Wish I'd seen you in it."

"Funny thing is, we had a lot of costumes. People think I'm kidding when I say that because all the publicity was about the nudity – and there was a lot of that – but I actually had five or six costume changes. The show was a lot of sketches, so each one was different characters…oh, I'm sure this is pretty boring."

"Hardly." He gets up, not taking his eyes off me, and goes to a small refrigerator near the desk, and takes out a bottle of white wine. "Cheap but good." It's already uncorked. He pours some into two plastic cups and hands one to me.

Not bad. With the coat around me, I feel safer, and kick off my platform heels, stretching my legs out in front of me. He watches my every move. This place is so quiet, I can hear his breathing. His grip on the gun relaxes a bit; at least he's not white-knuckling it like before. "I never thought I'd be in a show like that, not in a million years. But there was this audition, so I went. I sang, and learned some simple choreography, and read from a script, and figured that was that. But a few days later, they called me back. Asked me whether I had a problem with nudity. It didn't seem real and I couldn't imagine I'd get the job so what the hell. I sang again, I read again. They laughed and seemed to enjoy it. And then it was time for the naked part of the audition."

Chris sits up straighter.

"They cleared the theater, so it was just me, the director, the choreographer – a woman – and the stage manager. I was standing on this big empty stage. The director said, "We want you to improvise. You're walking through the woods, and come across a pond with clear water. It's a hot day, so you take off your clothes and wade into the water. It's warm and the sun is shining, and you think about someone you love, and say what you've wanted to say to them, as if you're writing a letter out loud.""

I take another sip of the wine. Chris downs his and pours another.

"It felt like a dream. I crossed the stage, imagining the sun shining down, the water, the fresh green grass and old trees. I kick off my shoes, then I start to take off my blouse – I was wearing a shiny, blue halter top and black slacks that day. I take the top off over my head and drop it. Then I push the slacks down, step out of them, and there I am in just a black push-up bra and bikini panties. Pink. I'm thinking I should have worn matching underwear. The bra closes in the front, so I unhook it and toss it on the floor of the stage. Slide the panties down and push them off with my foot. I feel the warm sun – it's just a stage light – and it reminds me of the Leonard Cohen lyric from 'Suzanne' about the sun being like honey. I kneel on the floor, facing the people in the audience, looking up at the 'sky.' Like I'm about to pray or something. A letter? Who should

I write to? There was a man I was seeing but he was married to someone else and my heart broke every day, so I composed my 'letter' to him, ending the relationship, like I should have done in real life. It felt like a weight was lifting off of me, like I really was floating under that sun, in that warm water, and everything was wonderful. I almost forgot I was auditioning. Or in a theater. Or that other people were there. I stood up, shaking the imaginary water off of me, felt it running down my body."

Christopher Fargate clears his throat, says in a whisper. "And?"

"And that was it."

"You got the part."

"I got the part." The memory is so vivid, I almost forget where I am now, in a grimy warehouse in Paris. "The show was already running and I was replacing an actress who was leaving. The rehearsals were a blur. Suddenly it was opening night, with all the panic and rushing around and worrying I'd forget my lines, or trip or sing a wrong note. The opening was when we all came downstage to music, wearing robes, then drop the robes. There we were. There I was, naked in front of a thousand strangers. And you know what I felt?"

He shakes his head.

"Fabulous!"

We both laugh. He looks at me for a long time. Then: "Becky—"

"Rebecca."

"Rebecca. I have a lot of money. I have a yacht, it's docked in Monaco right now. I want to travel around the world with... someone I care about. You could still make your records and have your career, and never have to worry about anything. I'm not really this person I'm pretending to be tonight. I just have to tie up a few loose ends and we'll both be free. Harry isn't coming back, you know that. We both know it. Think about it."

I pretend to think about it. He's right. Harry may not come back but I don't believe it. Then I do believe it. Then I don't. My head hurts.

It's been a long time since I've eaten, and the small amount of wine is blurring my thoughts. I've got to get out of here.

"Harry and I are finished anyway, whether he comes back or not. Tonight was the end of it, for both of us. It was just a fling." Taking a deep breath, trying to focus. "Tell me about that yacht."

"She's called Mona Lisa, but I'll rechristen her Rebecca. We'll have a marvelous life."

"But who do people think you are? If you're no longer Christopher Fargate."

He chuckles, pours some more wine. He offers the bottle but I shake my head. "Meet Jonathan Wooldridge III. Heir to an oil fortune. High stakes Baccarat player."

"Hello, Jonathan." I inch toward him, offering my hand. He recoils, gripping the gun. "Oh, are we still doing that? It'll be awkward sailing around Monaco while you're holding me at gunpoint. And I don't think they let you into the casinos packing a weapon."

"You think this is all a game, don't you?" His demeanor totally changes. "Do you really imagine I was serious?"

"What about that whole 'someone I care about' line of bullshit?"

"I was just playing along with your particular line of bullshit."

We regard each other. Two feral animals.

"Did you really imagine I'd go off with you? You aren't fit to clean Harry's boots."

He sneers, "Do you think I'm an idiot who's going to fall for your femme fatale routine? Like I'd want Harry Lamb's leftovers?"

There's a spinning sensation of some bright red light going off in my head, a rage rising up from beyond and beneath and within me, and without thinking I grab the heavy wooden chair I was sitting on and hurl it in Chris' direction. The chair glances off his shoulder, knocking him backwards. The gun goes off – a wild shot – and drops from his hand, sliding on the cement floor. We both dive for it, but I'm faster. I grab it. He lurches toward me. I grasp the gun with both hands, and shoot.

Striking him in the groin. He starts to speak, astonished, unable to comprehend what's happening. He groans, tries to stand, reaches toward me. "You fucking cunt!" I shoot again, straight into his chest. He's not yet dead but it's coming fast.

"Say hello to your pal, Alistair." Third shot straight to the face. His head explodes backwards, blood raining against the desk as he falls.

The body lying there. The gun in my hand. I'm trembling all over, even my teeth are vibrating. My heart is so loud it seems like it could explode. There's a creaking sound. Gripping the gun, I spin around. No one.

The radio. "*La neige tombe sur la mer....c'est la fin de l'affaire...*"

There's a bathroom in the back. I gulp water straight from the faucet and splash my face. I have to get out. But what if Harry comes back? I have no idea what time it is or how long Harry and the two men have been gone. We left the club at, what, two AM? The drive here…I can't pull my thoughts together. Think! Two more hours, maybe, since Harry left with the goons. Three hours. Is it getting light out yet? Maybe they killed Harry. What would he want me to do? I hear his voice in my head, as loud as if he were in the room. *Get the fuck out of there, Rebecca.*

I start to take off Chris's coat but realize my nightclub clothes would be more conspicuous than if I'm wearing a man's coat, and also I can put the gun in the pocket. It's all starting to make a kind of sense.

There's an exit door by the bathroom. I have to get my shoes and purse. There's nothing else of mine in the room. Is there? The paper cup and the plastic cup I drank out of, with lipstick on them. I stuff them into the coat pocket. Wouldn't I have left fingerprints? But where would anyone have my fingerprints to compare them to? Let *les flics* figure out what happened. Let them try to find me. I don't even exist here.

I have to step over a widening pool of blood. Nausea surges up from my gut to my throat. I swallow it back down, push the door open, and have a rush of panic that there could be an emergency alarm. No sound other than the thick door creaking. And the radio still playing, the singer's sorrowing voice of regret and snow and sad birds.

Bowl of Night

Still carrying my shoes and purse, I'm in some alley cluttered with trash cans. The end of the alley turns onto a street. It's deserted. Running barefoot, because putting on the stupid shoes will slow me down.

The air has turned cold with a light, spring frost on the ground and coating the trees. I pull the coat around me.

Something crunches under my foot. I recoil and hastily put on my shoes. An earthworm had crawled out from the ground – earlier in the day, perhaps, confused by a few hours of mild rain – and then had frozen. There are dozens of icicle earthworms; no, hundreds. I step over and around them, and then right on them, the crunch and crunch and crunch repulsive but somehow satisfying. Tears slide down my cheeks. It's much later – or earlier – than I thought. Car headlights flare in the silvery dawn. The Metro station is open! Looking like a woman slinking home from a one-night stand, I stagger down the Metro stairs and into the pungent warmth of a train.

44

With a generous advance from the record company, I check out of the Hotel le Bois, and rent a furnished apartment in Saint-Germain-des-Prés, not far from Max's place and the Alliance Française. It's two rooms and a kitchen, on the top floor of a four-story walk up, with a skylight and wide windows that look out over rooftops and a sliver of the Seine. It's the nicest place I've ever lived up till now. I even get a proper phone number; no more hotel desks or concierges taking messages for me. No more going to the street or a tabac to make a pay phone call.

Every day, I've bought French newspapers and a couple of the British ones. And every day, there is nothing about murders in Montmartre or at 22 rue Fleur. A week passes. Then another.

I call Max to give him my new phone number. He suggests we meet at Café de Flores, the haunt of Jean-Paul Sartre and Simone de Beauvoir (although I've never seen either of them there, let alone both.) He and Ellen are waiting when I arrive, each with a cappuccino. Ellen looks slimmer, more pulled together, and is genuinely friendly. She has a new boyfriend, a French doctor, and is extending her student visa. Max's English paramour has decamped back to Barcelona and I get the feeling it's over. Max asks if I ever found out what happened to Trish and the twins in Iran. I shake my head. I'd actually forgotten about them and Clementine, and should probably call her. *No, Alistair never showed up*, I hear myself telling Clementine. *Sorry.*

"…crazy thing in the paper," Ellen is saying, but I've lost the thread. "What?"

The waiter comes by and takes my order. Cappuccino.

Ellen reads, translating from the French. "The police found two dead bodies in an apartment in the 1st, you know, Louvre, and they seemed to have killed each other. But neither of them had any ID. It's a real mystery."

"You mean," Max says, "like a murder suicide? A husband wife thing?"

"No, two men. Although I suppose they could have been gay. Shot each other with two separate guns."

"How does that work?" Max laughs, "Like the OK Corral?" All three of us find this very funny. Then I can't stop laughing and they look at me like I'm crazy.

"Sorry, I…" I'm having trouble catching my breath. Max hands me a glass of water.

"But wait, it gets better," Ellen says, her eyes wide. "They found an*other* body in the 18th, and – get this – the guy had already been dead before, under another name!"

"The Man Who Died Twice," Max says. "Isn't that a movie?"

"If it isn't, it should be." Ellen skims down the page. "And they think these…deaths are connected somehow."

Max turns to me. "Are you all right? You're so pale."

"Fine. I'm fine, just tired, I guess." More water. "So, these people who died, who were they?"

"The one in Montmartre, with the other identity, was some art dealer who was supposed to have died months ago but had new ID. It came out when they got him to the morgue, and put down his name, one of the attendants said, no, that's this other guy. Or something like that. Geez, you can't make this stuff up."

"And the two at the other place?"

"Doesn't say much about them. No ID, I guess."

"But were they French?"

Ellen glances at me. "I don't know, why?"

The waiter brings my cappuccino, the white foam swirling like a hurricane. "No reason. I mean, they could be tourists."

Three men went into the apartment at 22 rue Fleur that night – two are dead.

Who was the third man?

Who lived, who died? If the chauffeur stayed outside, it would mean Harry was one of the dead men. But wouldn't I know if he were no longer on the earth? For an instant, the ground falls away, and I'm flying over the Iranian desert with Harry holding my hand, in that noisy yellow airplane.

Max is asking about my recording. I'm on automatic, with a parallel line of thought running in my head. Trying to work out the possibility of being implicated in these murders. I was in both places. My prints would be all over that apartment. But the men killed each other. Or someone set it up to look that way. No witnesses.

"The single should be out soon." But could there be witnesses? And if Harry isn't dead, where would he be? "They're going to release it in France, then the rest of Europe."

"That's fabulous!" Max says. He lifts his coffee cup in a toast.

Ellen joins him, a bit half-heartedly. "Yes. Congratulations."

"Doesn't mean it'll go anywhere. There are plenty of singers around." It's hard to believe that anything I'm doing could really be good. Although the demo has already been played at Sylvie's, giving me a small but select following.

Sylvie's. If Harry contacted me, that's where he'd do it. I haven't been back since the night of Chris Fargate.

45

One day you're a nobody, the next day you're a nobody with promise. You're in a hall of mirrors where every reflection is a disjointed part of you and you don't know which is real. Is it the girl with the wild hair riding through a field in the Midwest on some farmer's horse? The girl at church pretending to pray? The girl listening to her father holler at her brother that he's an idiot, a fake, a lost soul? Calling her a whore and a sinner?

There she is, the sinner and killer, the unsaved, the loved and lost, the talented, the loser, the shamed, the winner.

The survivor.

Making an entrance into the nonpareil nightspot as Somebody, for at least this fifteen minutes. Her demo is playing; everyone is dancing to it. Shouts of "Rebecca! Rebecca!" Or did I dream it all? Floating over to Sylvie des Anges and her blessed circle. The men getting up – one kisses my hand and offers a short, ironic bow. Will there ever be a time that Sylvie is not holding court in her cabaret castle? When we are no longer young? It seems impossible that time will wear us down. No, we are all here for eternity, suspended when we are at our peak.

Sylvie slips a small envelope into my hand. Overhead, the whirling crystal ball scatters shards of light throughout the room, turning the dancers into diamond fragments. I clutch the envelope, making my way towards the ladies' room in the back, where women in varying shades of transcendent beauty are freshening up, gossiping, giggling.

Ignoring them, I open it. Just a small slip of paper inside, with familiar handwriting.

You never know what will happen next.

I put it into my bag and rejoin the dancers.

FINIS

Acknowledgments

I want to thank my cat who likes to sit on the keyboard and gives me an excuse to stop writing and get a snack or rearrange a drawer. And the other cat who sits behind me like a lumbar support. And the third one who just meows a lot.

Big thanks to my wonderful editor, Rhonda Hayter, whose enthusiasm kept this book alive for me.

Appreciation for the fellow writers who offered input along the way: Kim Gottlieb-Walker, Ina S. Hillebrandt, Joan Jackson, Jovita Jenkins, Margaret Karlin, and Ellen Ruderman.

And much love and gratitude to my husband, Steve Kaplan, who reads my stuff and manages to live with me while staying relatively sane.

About the Author

Kathrin King Segal grew up in New York City. In her teens, she began singing and playing guitar in Greenwich Village, during the heyday of the folk scene. She soon turned to theater, appearing in numerous Off- and Off-Off Broadway plays and musicals, and one notorious Broadway show. In 1991, her first novel, *Wild Again*, was published by Dutton/Penguin.

Kathrin and her husband moved to Los Angeles, where she continued to write and perform. Her second novel, *We Were Stardust*, explores the burgeoning pop and folk-rock music world in the 1960s, from the Village to L.A. Having delved into the '60s and '80s, it seemed time to check out the 1970s in *Bowl of Night*. She's working on a new novel set in the present, as well as a memoir that covers many of the remaining decades. She's also released two CDs of mostly original songs. The novels and CDs can be found on her Amazon page and her website, www.KathrinKingSegal.com.

Over her lifetime, Kathrin has been, in no particular order: actor, receptionist, dog walker, singer, cotton-factory material folder, autodidact, go-go dancer, story analyst, songwriter, manic depressive, switchboard operator, songwriter, cat rescuer, journalist, horse rider, wife, trypophobe, cancer survivor, feeder of neonatal kittens, and writer of books.

She lives in beautiful Chatsworth, California with her husband and three cats, and enjoys traveling the world when there isn't a pandemic.